Promises in Courage

To Julie - dear friend -
So glad to know you -
Thanks for your support
and beautiful smile!

DeAnn Kruempel

DEANN KRUEMPEL

COPYRIGHT INFORMATION

Promises in Courage
First published in United States by BOEKERBOOKS
2741 Kraft Lane, Missouri Valley, Iowa 51555

www.boekerbooks.com
Tell your story.

Text Copyright © DeAnn Kruempel 2019.

Produced by Nathan Boeker.
Cover design by Dead Simple Design.
Cover image by luizclas/pexels
Text and layout by BOEKERBOOKS.

ISBN-13: 9781702802543

CONTENTS

To laugh often and much;
To win the respect of intelligent people
and the affection of children;
To earn the appreciation of honest critics
and endure the betrayal of false
friends;
To appreciate beauty, to find the best in
others;
To leave the world a bit better whether by
a healthy child, a garden patch, or a
redeemed social condition;
To know even one life has breathed easier
because you have lived.
This is to have succeeded.

~ Ralph Waldo Emerson

Promises in Courage

JOURNAL OF LYDI ANNA ANDERSSON

NOVEMBER 27, 1939

It did not happen suddenly. No, it has taken a year and a half to reach this point, but finally my heart does not hurt anymore. There has been a long period of sadness and worry.

I still really miss my dad, though, and I cry sometimes, thinking how he only got to begin his dream of having our own farm. Michael and I have tried to be brave and to keep our promises to him, but it has not been easy, especially when Mom withdrew into her own grief after he died. I am so glad Michael and I had Grandma to help us take care of the animals and the garden, and dear friends and neighbors, William and Geoffrey, to help with the harvest. We were all so relieved when Mom finally overcame her time of isolation, but then we faced the possible loss of the farm because there was not enough money to make the payment that year. I was scared that we would have to leave this place, and I did not know what we would do or where we would go. I knew Michael would be devastated. But we all worked together and managed to come up with the money.

For a long time I have been afraid to dream, to look forward, to truly feel happiness about anything, because at any time I was afraid it would be torn away. My heart must be healing, though, for tonight I feel an excitement about the future that I have not experienced for a long time.

Just a month until Christmas. I love the decorating, the baking, making presents secretly and then hiding them. Mom and I are going to make lefse. She wants to give some as gifts to her friends. It will take five pounds of potatoes just to make enough for

Michael! He loves the flat circles of potato bread with butter and sugar.

Grandma has invited me to come over and learn to sew on her new sewing machine. William bought her a new Singer that runs with a treadle. She says it takes practice to learn how to coordinate the treadle with the wheel and needle. I hope I can learn to use it. I want to sew a new apron for Mom and a pillowcase for Michael.

Grandma and William were married a few weeks ago. I miss having her here, but it is fun to visit them, and it is obvious they are very happy. Grandpa William's brother, Geoffrey, teases the newlyweds mercilessly, and there is always laughter in their home.

I am especially excited for spring! AmyBelle, our Jersey cow, and Michael's black sheep, Dottie, are to have babies. I am picturing an adorable baby lamb and a calf frolicking through the pasture. Michael can hardly wait! Almost eight, my little brother is already setting up his farm with live-stock, and he loves those animals dearly.

There is gossip that Dr. Evans and his wife Becky are expecting a child, too. I hope all will go well. Working with Dr. Evans at his office has taught me a lot about people and medicine. Since Dad died, it has become my dream to become a doctor. I read every book and article I can get my hands on about disease, healing and prevention. My family, Miss Johnston, our teacher, and my friends at school all encourage me. "Don't give up!" they tell me. "Follow your dream."

I cannot imagine doing anything else. Life is exciting and it feels good to have hope again. I have so much to look forward to.

L. A. A.

Promises in Courage

CHAPTER 1

THE PEDDLER

"The journey to America was not easy for many European immigrants. The passengers who had little money were packed into the ship's steerage compartment, below the decks. This is where they lived, sleeping, eating and braving the two to three months in relative darkness. Limited sanitation, dirty water and rats contributed to disease and death. Typhus and cholera were prevalent. Sometimes families attempting the crossing lost a child or parent." Benjamin sighed and shook his head after reading from the textbook during the history lesson.

"Thank you, Benjamin." Miss Johnston's gaze swept over her one-room school. Though classes were conducted at the recitation bench for each class level, often the others in the room listened to the lessons. "For what reasons did people from Europe want to come to the United States?"

Ethel raised her hand to answer. "The Irish came because of the potato famine. They had no food and no way to make a living."

"Religious freedom," contributed Mabel after a nod from Miss Johnston. "And some were so poor they just wanted a better life."

"Excellent, class. When you go home tonight you might ask your families from what countries your ancestors came. There may be some interesting stories." Miss Johnston often encouraged her students to enrich their studies at home. Hearing a stifled sob from Vicky, who sat next to her twin brother in the front row with the youngest group, Miss Johnston hurried to the child's desk. She knelt down next to the four-year old. "Vicky, what is wrong? Why are you crying?"

"Do you think any twins came over on those *imgrent* ships? If their mommy or daddy died, that would be just awful. Our mommy died when we was borned, but what if we lost Daddy, too?" Tears flowed from the little girl's eyes as the teacher put her arm around the child's shoulders. Ricky reached for his sister's hand and, though he tried to subdue his own tears, the look of total sadness on his face betrayed him.

Miss Johnston stood. "Students, you have worked hard this morning. Thank you for all of your excellent answers. Let's dismiss a few minutes early for our lunch period. Please remember your jackets," she prompted as the youngsters began filing out of the room.

Though the teacher's relationship with the Christleton twins went beyond being their teacher, she reminded herself that her responsibility at the Chaucer Township School was to all of the children. "What did your daddy pack for your lunch this morning, Ricky?" The three started to the front entry of the school where lunches were stored on a table and wraps were hung on hooks.

Suddenly Maximus opened the front door and peeked in. "Teacher, the crippled man is here! The peddler!"

"Crippled man?" Shock and sympathy replaced the sadness in Vicky's eyes.

"He does have a disability, Vicky. He has no legs." Miss Johnston took the children's small hands in hers and walked out to greet the peddler who had been visiting her school twice a year since she started teaching.

The man drove a white vehicle that looked like a combination of a car and a pickup. All was enclosed with windows to allow easy viewing of the car's contents. Items for sale were organized into groups and included kitchen supplies of plastic containers, small baskets, cooking utensils and kettles. There was a compartment with books, various school supplies and toys and games. Hats, scarves, mittens and stockings were displayed on small shelves just behind the driver, and an assortment of watches and jewelry sparkled on hangers and dowels in what would have been the front passenger seat.

The children were milling around the peddler's vehicle. They greeted him through the open windows. He called a greeting to Miss Johnston as she and the twins approached. Ricky joined the other young boys as they curiously checked out the store on wheels. Vicky clung to Miss Johnston's hand as she cautiously stepped near the driver's window and stared in at the peddler.

"Hello, Mr. Mackey. It is good to see you. The students are enjoying your visit to our school." Miss Johnston smiled as she perused the school supply compartment. "This is Vicky. She and her brother are new at school this year. Vicky, this is Mr. Mackey."

The man smiled and slowly reached a hand out to the small child who placed her hand in his. "Nice to meet you, young lady. I bet you are as smart as you are pretty."

"I don't know 'bout that, but Daddy says I am pre-co-cious, whatever that means." The child took a hesitant step forward, keeping her eyes on the man.

"Will you excuse me, Mr. Mackey? I need to run inside and get my pocketbook." Miss Johnston bent down to Vicky. "Why don't you walk around to the other side and look at the hair ribbons." The woman gave the child a gentle nudge, but Vicky remained fixed to her spot.

"That's a nice looking glove, Mr. Mackey." Benjamin peeked into the opposite window as he pointed to a baseball glove hanging from a hanger fastened to the roof. The man reached for a smooth wooden stick with a small hook on the end, adeptly clasped the glove, then tossed it to Benjamin.

"Try it on, young man. See how it fits your hand."

"Mr. Mack?" Vicky spoke, her head tipped back, chin nearly touching the smooth paint on the car.

"Do you have a question for me, Miss Vicky?"

"Miss Johnston said you don't have legs. How can you drive a car without legs?"

A bit surprised by the child's abrupt question, the man glanced downward, but then he replied with a gentle smile, "That's a good question, little lady! I've got me two sons, each one as smart as a whip, and they built this car just for me. One is a carpenter, and he made all the displays and shelves. The other is a mechanic, and he made all the controls to work with hands instead of feet. Runs slick as a whistle, and I just sit here."

Lydi, Ethel and Mabel were circling around, peering into each window. Their eyes met, and they grinned as they heard the man's patient explanation to Vicky.

All at once the four-year-old drew in a breath and her eyes grew round, as if the most earth-shattering thought had just occurred to her. "Mr. Mack," the child whispered, "if you don't have any legs to walk on, then how do you go…"

"OH, Vicky!" Ethel rushed to the little girl's side before she could finish her obvious question and directed a look of apology to the peddler. "Let's go find Ricky, I bet he found a present for you somewhere in there." She whisked Vicky away, leaving Lydi and Mabel, embarrassed at the child's personal question.

Lydi leaned forward to apologize and noticed that the man was shaking. She worried for a second, wondering if the child's open curiosity had offended the man. Then she realized he was trying to control his laughter. Tears of mirth were running down his face. "Girl, no need to apologize for the little one. She was just curious." He dried the tears on his cheeks with a red bandanna, and shook his head, still chuckling. "I don't think I have ever been asked THAT before!"

Just then Miss Johnston hastened to the peddler's car with her pocketbook in hand. She saw him wipe his eyes. "Oh, Mr. Mackey, I do hope the children have not offended you in any way."

The man's twinkling eyes met Lydi's and he winked. "No, Ma'am. The children have been just fine."

Promises in Courage

CHAPTER 2

IMAGES

"…and every one of us got a stick of Juicy Fruit gum! How can he do that? Nobody bought anything except Miss Johnston." Michael chattered about the peddler's visit as he reached for another slice of rye bread that evening at the family supper table.

"It makes good business sense to keep people happy, don't you think?" Anna contributed. "How many of those children went home and told their parents about the peddler? They will be prepared for his visit and probably plan to buy an item or two if they can. They might even purchase a few Christmas gifts."

"Yeah, I s'pose." Still chewing, Michael added another helping of potatoes to his plate. "I wonder if he lost his legs in the war."

Lydi had remained silent during much of the meal. The image of the man and how he coped with his situation kept churning through her mind. Finally she spoke. "I cannot help but think of how awful it must have been for him at first. How must he have felt?"

"No kidding! Do you think he just woke up and realized he would never walk again? Never be able to do all the fun stuff he used to?" Michael shook his head and looked down at his supper, not as appealing as a few seconds ago.

"But he handles everything, takes life in stride as though he is not all that different from anyone else. Vicky's questions did not seem to bother him a bit. He was laughing!" Lydi's eyes met her mother's. "How could anyone have such courage?"

Anna sighed, but smiled gently at her daughter. "I am sure it took time for the man to adjust, to come to terms with his plight and decide how to deal with it. It is what we must do in life." A look of sadness flashed across the woman's face as she remembered her family's loss, less than two years ago.

"I don't know." Michael stared into his glass of milk, his vivid imagination at work. "I don't think I could handle it. If I didn't have legs, I couldn't take care of Dottie and Star. I wouldn't be able to clean their stalls or run with them in the pasture." He shook his head and, eyes glistening, his gaze met Lydi's. "If Dottie had trouble havin' her lamb, I could not even help her. That'd be just awful."

"But, like the peddler, you would learn to cope with it, Michael. You would persevere. Remember Dad taught us that we should never give up, no matter what."

"Maybe, Lydi, but thinking about it now I wonder if I could do it." He paused for a moment. "No, I think I might just rather die." His voice cracked as he spoke.

The devastation on her brother's face wrenched Lydi's heart. Though she had felt similar emotions, her brother's comment bothered her, and she did not know why. Could anything ever be that bad?

Promises in Courage

CHAPTER 3

BILLIE'S CHRISTMAS VISIT

Letter in hand, Ethel came running to meet Lydi as she arrived at school on Monday. "Lydi, you are not going to believe this!" she called.

"What is it, Ethel? Is it another letter from Billie?" Lydi had come to admire Ethel's cousin, Billie, who was a coal miner's daughter in Baldwin, Colorado. The girl and her family, who lived in a mining camp, were at the mercy of the owners, and barely had enough money to make ends meet. Billie wrote letters to Ethel, who shared them with her friends. Lydi had begun to write to Billie and felt a kinship with the girl, though they had never met face-to-face.

"Yes, a letter, and guess what? She's coming on the train to visit! You will get to meet her!" Ethel threw her arms around her friend and they nearly danced with excitement.

"But, she cannot come alone on the train, and how will her family afford the fare?" Lydi questioned in disbelief.

"Do you remember her teacher, Miss Nelson? She has a sister in Omaha and plans to visit her the week before Christmas. She offered to travel with Billie to the train depot in Council Bluffs, and then they will meet again just before Christmas and ride the train back to Colorado. That way Miss Nelson and Billie will be back home to celebrate Christmas."

"Oh, my, it seems almost too good to be true! I will finally get to meet Billie." Lydi's eyes glowed with excitement.

"Billie says the ticket cost has been taken care of. I am just glad she can come." Ethel presented the letter to her friend with a flourish and smiled while she read.

"She will arrive on Sunday, December 17th, the same day as the Christmas program at school." Ethel smiled expectantly at her younger friend and went on. "So, she will meet everyone that night, and then we have four more days to do whatever we want! Mom and Esther will be at work, so we will have time to ourselves. I hope you can come visit."

Lydi thought for a second and then suggested, "Maybe we can come and pick you and Billie up and you can come to my house. Or Grandma would love to serve us all tea. Billie will have to meet Michael's Dottie and Star and see all the animals on the farm. Oh, Ethel, I can hardly wait!"

"I knew you would be delighted, Lydi. I will write back to Billie and make sure all the travel arrangements will work."

Lydi clasped her hands, holding them against her heart. Her eyes turned up to the billowy white clouds as they scuttled beyond the school's bell tower. "Another thing to look forward to. Ethel, this is going to be the best Christmas ever! I don't want anything to spoil our plans."

Promises in Courage

Promises in Courage

CHAPTER 4

THE EXAMINATION

A gray Model 40 Ford was parked in the schoolyard driveway next to Miss Johnston's car. Covered in brown dust, it looked like it had seen its way down some Iowa dirt roads. As the students arrived this Friday in early December, they noticed the extra vehicle but carried on playing on the swings or merry-go-round or talking with friends until Miss Johnston came out of the schoolhouse door to ring the bell.

Lydi and her friends, Ethel, Mabel, Lilly and Julia walked in together. They left their lunch pails on the table in the entry, then removed their coats and hung them on the hooks on the wall. Ethel had remained quieter than usual outside, and Lydi noticed a troubled frown on her friend's face. "Hey, is there something on your mind? You look worried."

Ethel released a heavy sigh, then whispered. "Do you think this might be the new teacher to replace Miss Johnston when she marries?"

"No, Ethel. Miss Johnston was confident that you would be approved for the position as long as you agreed to finish normal school while you teach. This must be someone else. Don't worry!" Lydi patted the girls arm and they strode together into the one room school.

The teacher stood and waited for all the students to file to their desks before she addressed the class in a serious tone. "Today is a very important day for us, students. Before I explain and introduce our special visitor, we will say the Pledge of Allegiance. Lilly, will you please lead us?"

Moments later an air of uneasiness hovered over the students as they shuffled into their seats and glanced about for clues of what was to come. At last, Miss Johnston cleared her throat and waited for her class's silent attentiveness. "Thank you, all of you. Today we have an important guest visiting us. This is Miss Kipling, the County Superintendent of Schools." Miss Johnston gestured to the woman sitting primly at the table in the corner of the room. "She will speak with you first and then administer examinations to every grade level. Please give her your complete attention and then do your very best."

The visitor was middle-aged, tall and thin. Her light brown hair, streaked with gray, was pulled into a tight bun at the back of her head. She wore a gray suit that came far below her knees. Her blouse matched the suit exactly and, tucked under the starched gray collar was a shiny black ribbon that made a bow in front. Simple black pumps clunked on the wooden floor as the woman walked purposefully to the front of the room, then turned to face the group.

Eyes sweeping over each child, Miss Kipling did not smile. "Students. I am here to administer examinations today, as Miss Johnston said. I will begin with the tests for the younger groups. Then I will speak to the older students and oversee their test. Grades kindergarten through four please move to this part of the room." She pointed to her right.

Miss Johnston observed as her younger students filed to the indicated area, all except Vicky and Ricky. Vicky was holding her twin brother's hand, but he remained glued to his seat. He was trembling. The teacher's heart went out to the little ones, but she knew she must not approach them, for this test was not in her control. Ethel tried to get their attention, but she was sitting just behind them. Finally Vicky coaxed Ricky into standing. Hand-in-hand they turned, and as they looked back they met Ethel's eyes. She gave them the warmest smile she could muster and nodded to them. Somewhat reassured, Ricky released his sister's hand and the two made their way hesitantly to the remaining desks.

Miss Kipling's expression remained stoic. Ethel waited for a reprimand, for she knew the superintendent had seen the exchange, but none was given.

A pencil and test were placed in front of each young child. "We will begin with the arithmetic exam. Each student will be graded according to his or her class level. Just answer the problems you can and do your best. You may begin."

Directly, the woman turned to the older group. "Students." Her concise, no-nonsense approach allowed no digression. "Today all forty-four Iowa County Superintendents are monitoring these examinations across the state. Our purpose is to determine your class placement, and, of course, see how you are advancing in this classroom." She made a point to turn her face to Miss Johnston, as though there was more on the line this day than the students' progress. There was not a sound as the woman continued. "Also, this year, the top ten scholars in the state will receive a $100 check from the Bayir Pharmaceutical Company. Bayir and

Johns Hopkins University have partnered to encourage more young people to pursue a higher education. The awards will be presented by Governor Wilson at the capitol building in April." Finished with instructions, Miss Kipling placed a test in front of each of the students, upside down on their desks.

One hundred dollars! The amount was staggering to Lydi, and just for a moment a flicker of hope flashed through her mind. She immediately smothered it. No, I have no chance of scoring higher than so many students who are older and have completed more advanced classes. I will not even think of winning, for it will only cause more stress. The other girls in the group may have had similar thoughts, for they glanced at each other and nodded in silent encouragement.

Suddenly Lydi's gaze met Benjamin Hindricks, their eyes locking for several seconds. Then Benjamin flashed his heart-stopping smile and mouthed the words, "Good Luck!" Lydi willed her mouth to move, to whisper, "you, too," but it refused to obey. At last she looked away, for she was certain that her face had blushed to the color of neighbor Geoffrey's pink roses. Her heart was singing.

"Students, are you ready to take your examination?"

Lydi Anna Andersson was quite certain at that moment she was ready to take on the world.

Promises in Courage

CHAPTER 5

VERMIN!

Evening shadows had vanished as Lydi hurried to the barn to take care of the chickens. The red sunset was a thumbnail on the horizon, its pink halo dipping down behind the lone cottonwood that stood next to the building. Bare gnarled branches dimmed the light and for a moment the sun seemed tangled in a dark web. Reaching the door the girl noticed a movement up in the tree and stopped to watch. A single leaf dangled about half-way up, twisting and thrashing like a prisoner trying desperately to escape her tethers. Lydi shivered as a gust of wind swept down the hill. The golden heart fluttered wildly, but the branch held on.

The small west windows on the barn allowed just enough remaining sunlight to see the pens and storeroom that surrounded the central room. The chickens were already singing their sleep song. Dottie and Star bleated and peeked between the boards on their pen. Lydi gave each of their hard bony heads a scratch, then searched for the water bucket. Bless Michael! He had left it filled for her when he did his chores. No need to run out to the pump. She reached down to find the handle and felt something brush against her hand! Startled, she jumped back with a shriek. There was a brief flash of eyes, then Lydi heard a shuffle of movement to the storeroom wall.

Grabbing the bucket again, she hurried into the chickens' pen, partitioned with netted wire that was nailed to two by fours that reached up to the floor of the haymow above. She filled the water trough, then peered into the settling darkness for what may still be lurking there. The feed was in the storeroom and the chickens needed their rations. Uttering a silent prayer, the girl moved stealthily through the middle room, to the storeroom. She quickly opened the bins, scooped out the grain and slammed the cover back down. Back in the main room she hesitated. Listened. There was only the sound of the sheep munching on the hay in the manger and the chickens crooning. With a sense of relief she quickly returned to the chicken coop, poured the grain into the feeders and gathered the eggs from the straw-lined nests.

Seven brown eggs nestled in the center of her apron as she grasped the bottom corners in her left hand. Again, Lydi stopped in the middle area to peer and listen after closing the chicken coop door. Then she saw them. Eyes. Two sets of beady eyes glowed red from the reflection of the last remnants of sun peeking through the windows. The eyes followed her as she crept through the open room, but they did not move from the floor next to the bins. She dropped the water bucket and ran to the door.

As she was pushing the door shut, she had to look back. The eyes were still watching.

Apron swinging wildly in front of her, Lydi raced all the way back to the house.

Promises in Courage

CHAPTER 6

THE BATTLE BEGINS

"Rats!" William and Grandma and Geoffrey visited the next day after hearing Lydi's report of creatures in the barn. "They have gnawed a hole in the corner of the storeroom door. Looks like they found the corn." William led the others through the barn, all looking for evidence of the animals that had startled the girl. "They are rodents and like to, actually need to, chew because their pair of incisor teeth are constantly growing."

"They are social creatures, so most likely there is more than one or two. They are nocturnal so we are unlikely to see them today." Geoffrey, who had been reading since he was four, added to his brother's comments. "A group of rats is called a 'mischief.' Ironically, a group of crows, who are quite harmless, is termed a 'murder.'"

"Right now the word murder sounds appropriate. I don't ever want to have to deal with them again," declared Lydi. "They were creepy."

"Neither rats nor their excrement should be near farm animals or food sources. They have been known to carry deadly disease and parasites. Michael, young lad, this will be a lesson for you in your farming career; we need to formulate a plan to rid these rodents from the premises." William patted the young boy on his shoulder.

"What do I have to do, Grandpa William? Should I trap 'em?" Though only seven, the boy took his farm very seriously.

William glanced at his twin brother, as though checking to make sure they were in agreement. He leaned down to address Michael eye to eye. "Geoffrey and I usually concur that animals should be managed as humanely as possible. Perchance, the rats can be encouraged to vacate your barn. Geoffrey is quite adept at producing concoctions. If the rats' olfactory senses were to be over-stimulated, they may choose to seek a new residence."

At the words "olfactory senses" Grandma lifted her eyes heavenward and mouthed, "Heaven, help us!"

Seeing the confused look on Michael's face, Geoffrey explained, "Olfactory refers to the sense of smell, lad. Placing materials throughout the barn that the rodents find repulsive may drive them out."

"This smelly stuff won't hurt Dottie or Star, will it? Dottie is in the family's way, and I have to protect her, you know." Michael pulled his boot through the loose dirt on the barn floor, creating a swirl. "And I don't want anything to happen to Star or the chickens."

"The preparation assuredly will not harm the livestock. They may even fancy the aroma," Geoffrey replied, eyebrows lifting up and down in mischief.

"We shall endeavor to coax the rats to leave first. If that fails, we may need to resort to other methods." William turned to his brother. "Geoffrey always has enjoyed a challenge."

"Indubitably," agreed Geoffrey with a mischievous grin as he eagerly rubbed his hands together.

Promises in Courage

CHAPTER 7

THE DONATION JAR

Ever since the peddler's visit, Vicky and Ricky had bombarded their father, Greg, and Miss Johnston with questions. "How do people get crippled? What if a kid gets crippled and he has no mommy or daddy—who helps him?" Finally the teacher decided it might make the twins feel better to help do something for children with disabilities.

"Students, before we begin class this morning, I want to tell you about this jar." The woman finished tying a red and green ribbon around the neck of a mason jar and placed it on the front of her desk. The clear glass vessel had a slot cut into the cover and a neatly lettered label across the front which read, "Crippled Children's Home."

"When I was a young student like you, each year at Christmas our class chose a special project to support, and the teacher set out a jar much like this. We all brought whatever change we could, and at Christmas my teacher would send that money to the charity or a person who needed help. We always felt like we had a part in making someone's Christmas a little brighter."

Miss Sally Johnston looked around her classroom. She saw threadbare shirts, dresses that had grown too short and holes in the toes of shoes. These children, along with their parents, were survivors. They had lived through the Great Depression, the dust storms, the grasshoppers that wiped out everything in their path. They knew what it was like to go hungry. For a moment the teacher wondered if she was expecting too much from these families who were still recovering from hard times.

A small hand shot up and waved back and forth in excitement. "Yes, Vicky?" Miss Johnston granted the young child permission to speak.

"My Daddy gives me a nickel sometimes when I help with dishes. I've got a bunch of nickels in my piggy bank. I'm gonna open it up and bring some of them."

The other students smiled and nodded encouragement to the girl. At that moment, Miss Johnston knew that every student in her school would bring something to add to the jar. She told them how very proud she was of them, and in spite of her warm smile, few missed their teacher's glistening eyes or the catch in her voice.

Promises in Courage

CHAPTER 8

TREADLE TROUBLE

Geoffrey added another handful of herbs to the large kettle heating on the woodstove, then stirred gently with a long wooden spoon. Curls of steam rose from the pot and the man sniffed, eyes closed, as if savoring the aroma. "Ah, yes, my little concoction is approaching perfection. Those loathsome rats will be driven away by the distinct odor. I am certain of it."

Christina cast a pointed look at Lydi, for they had discussed Geoffrey's potions and the resulting smells that often lingered in her kitchen following his medicinal endeavors. "That is fine, Geoffrey, but will it also drive the humans out of my kitchen?" The woman questioned her brother-in-law seriously, though Lydi saw the gleam in her grandmother's eyes. "Lydi and I are going to the sewing room before we are overcome with fumes."

Geoffrey's burst of laughter filled the room. "Good luck with the sewing machine, Lydi. Brother William has yet to master it!"

Grandma's new Singer sewing machine sat in the corner of the room, near the north window. The shiny black top was adorned with gold lettering and flowing leaves that covered the front. A small wheel was attached to the right of the machine body which rested on a dark wooden desk. Below the small wheel, close to the floor was a much larger circle that reminded Lydi of a steering wheel. Under the machine, a few inches from the floor was a flat brass platform with oval holes that were similar to the holes on the two wheels. It rested on a metal bar that ran the length of the cabinet, and could move up and down like a pedal. This was the treadle.

"Oh, Lydi, a sewing machine is such a wonderful invention. I can sew strips of quilt blocks in a few minutes. Remember how many hours it took to stitch them together by hand?" Grandma ran her fingers lovingly over the smooth surface.

"Yes, Grandma. You sat in your rocker stitching those quilt blocks many winter evenings." The girl surveyed the machine apprehensively. "Do you think I will be able to learn how to use it? It looks complicated."

"Of course, child. If I can do it, so can you. The trick is to use your hand on the top wheel to get started. Then, of course, to move your foot on the treadle to keep it going. That is what makes the needle go up and down in the fabric. You will learn quickly, I know it." The older woman pulled the bench out and reached for a scrap of fabric. "Now, you sit down and practice."

Lydi slipped onto the seat as she released a sigh of pent-up excitement. There would be so many things she could make. Mom and Grandma would no longer need to sew her dresses and aprons. She could help with quilts and sewing Michael's shirts. Placing the cotton print carefully under the pressure foot, her grandmother showed her how to lower the foot so that the needle and thread could make secure stitches.

"Now place your foot on the treadle and your right hand on the wheel over here," the woman instructed as she touched the side wheel. "First, turn the wheel with your hand and then immediately pump the treadle up and down. See what happens."

Lydi started the machine with her hand and tried to move her foot. There were three clicks and the needle stopped in the material. "Sometimes it takes a while to get it going. Try it again." Grandma moved a high backed chair to sit close.

A frown of determination on her face, the girl went through the actions again, this time forcing the treadle harder as her hand flew from the side wheel down to the fabric in front of the needle. Again, the needle moved up and down a few times and then stuck. She puffed out a sigh of frustration and turned to Grandma. Smiling kindly, the woman patted her granddaughter's arm. "Remember what Geoffrey said? William has yet to master sewing. It just takes practice, Dear."

Another resolute effort with the treadle failed and Lydi's face fell to her chest. She slapped both hands down on her knees. "I can't do it, Grandma! It is as though my foot will not move the treadle like it is supposed to."

"Sometimes we make things more difficult when we try so hard. You are doing fine, Lydi. Let's take a break and we will try again in a bit. Maybe Geoffrey has finished in the kitchen," the older woman consoled, wondering at Lydi's unusual impatience.

The young girl followed her grandmother, but devastation emanated from her whole being. Grandma poured water into her basin and said cheerfully, "I guess it does not smell too dreadful in here. You just sit and I will finish these dishes."

"I will help you," Lydi found the dishtowel, but silence hovered over the two like a heavy cloud. She carefully pushed the towel into a tall drinking glass and twisted it to dry the inside. Suddenly the glass crashed to the floor, shattering into jagged fragments. "Oh, Grandma, I am so sorry!" She bent to pick up the pieces. "I will replace it for you."

Christina stooped to help. "It is all right. We have more glasses. Just be careful not to get cut."

Lydi tried to stand to put the larger pieces of glass on the counter and fell back to her knee. "OH!" Tears of exasperation flowed from her eyes as she finally pulled herself up next to a chair. "I just need to go home. I am sorry." She teetered for a moment, then with great effort, moved to the door and struggled to open it.

Her brows turned down in worry, the grandmother watched as the girl faltered home. "Something is wrong," she lamented quietly to herself. "Something is dreadfully wrong."

Promises in Courage

CHAPTER 9

CHAPTER 9

A MOTHER'S WORST NIGHT-MARE

Anna Andersson stood quietly and studied the sleeping girl in front of her. A flashback pulsed through her mind of the same child as a tiny baby in her bassinet. The memory warmed her heart. Was it really 12 years ago?

Today, Lydi was not resting peacefully. She laid on her side with her back against the davenport and her knees drawn up. Her arms were bent at the elbow and clenched tightly against her sides. Her small hands were laced together in front of her face, as if in prayer. With each jagged breath the girl's brows turned down and her eyes squeezed shut. A slight whimper escaped from deep in her throat every few seconds.

Instinctively, the mother moved to her child. She sidled next to her daughter on the couch and rested her hand on the girl's side. Immediately, she felt heat emanate from the child's body. She leaned over and softly spoke, "Lydi. Lydi, are you all right?"

The young girl's head thrashed from side to side before she finally opened her eyes and tried to focus on her mother. "I am sorry, Mom. I don't know what is wrong with me. I ache all over." The words came slowly in a hoarse whisper. Then she turned her face, opened one hand and straightened her arm. "I need to get to the barn to help Michael."

"Michael can finish the chores tonight, Lydi. Let's just try and get you feeling better. Come to the kitchen while I start supper. I will make you some tea." Anna forced a smile, stood, and took her daughter's hand in her own to help her up.

Lydi held the hand weakly and reached for the edge of the couch with her other. Anna felt a slight tug, but then stillness. All at once the girl's hand trembled violently. Her panic-stricken eyes flew to her mother's. "I cannot move, Mom! My legs won't move!"

With a calmness she did not feel, the mother assured the girl that she would be fine in the morning, after a good night's rest. "Lydi, I am going to have Michael stay with you while I drive to town and get Dr. Evans. We will just have him check you to make sure everything is all right."

A sliver of orange, a remnant of the sunset, wrestled with the cottonwood limbs, but cast a meager light as Anna turned her blue Ford pickup toward Canterbury. Worry loomed over her, and the wound that had scarred her heart since losing her husband, threatened to rip open. She did not know if she could bear to lose Lydi, too. Gloom began inching

its way into her soul, but the woman pressed forward. Finally, the sun's signature was snuffed out
by darkness.

Promises in Courage

CHAPTER 10

THE DIAGNOSIS

The doctor avoided the mother's eyes as he walked into the kitchen. She sat at the small table, both hands clutching the teacup in front of her, as if drawing strength from its warmth. He carried the tea kettle from the warmer on the back of the cook stove to the basin in the sink, poured the hot liquid, reached for the bar of lye soap on the counter and began scrubbing his hands. Anna watched in silence, wondering how long it took to scrub whatever germs might lurk on a doctor's skin after examining a patient.

After what seemed forever to the woman, he sat across from her, drew in a deep breath and met her eyes. "We need to get Lydi to the hospital, Anna. I will make arrangements at the Council Bluffs facility and come back early in the morning to take her there."

Though questions screamed inside her, she waited without speaking.

"Michael should be kept away from her, as well as anyone else. Lydi must be kept in isolation."

Anna stared at the man in front of her as though he was a stranger, threatening her life.

"You will need to come with me to sign papers at the hospital, but then we must leave her there for treatment. No one will be allowed to visit for some time."

The thought of not being able to comfort her child when she was suffering terribly spurred Anna to reality. "No, I cannot leave her there alone! I will stay with her. I don't care what sickness she has, or if I am in danger, I will help her through this." She stood then, but leaned on the table with both hands, daring this man to challenge a mother's love for her child.

He spoke softly, meeting her gaze with compassion. "Anna, I understand your need to be with Lydi, but with this illness the hospital's rules will not allow it. It seems cruel to both the child and parent, but strict regulations must be enforced to keep the dreadful virus from spreading."

Tears filled her eyes and she sat again, waiting for the diagnosis, bracing herself for the terrifying words she was about to hear.

The physician gently placed his hand on hers as she clenched them in front of her. "Anna, Lydia has polio."

Promises in Courage

CHAPTER 11

THE LONGEST RIDE

Fe...Fi...Fo...Fum! The giant's massive strides pounded in her brain. She remembered her father reading "Jack and the Beanstalk" with so much expression, she could almost feel the earth shake. At this moment Lydi wondered if the goliath had actually kidnapped her.   The jolt from each step pounded through her body. From her toes on up, the pain seared like fire, then settled in her head, flaring with each beat of her heart.

"I know this must hurt terribly, Lydi, but I am being as careful as I can. We need to get you to a hospital." Dr. Evans walked slowly and evenly as he carried the young girl to his car. Michael opened the car door and stood, waiting. The man motioned for the boy to stand back, but Lydi saw the misery in her brother's eyes. She wanted to tell him it would be okay, but the crushing pain would not allow her to speak.

With her mother's help, she was positioned on the back seat. Forcing herself to appear calm, Anna hugged Michael and crawled in the passenger side. As the car turned from the lane onto the gravel road, Lydi thought she heard the doctor say the word "polio." Her mind churned for a moment, for she remembered reading about polio, but her brain gave in to her body's demand for rest, and she drifted into merciful sleep.

The doctor glanced to the back seat, hoping Lydi would be awake enough for him to prepare her somewhat for what lay ahead. For the mother's sake he began to explain. "Polio is a virus, actually a virus of three types. Each can affect the patient differently. The first type causes paralysis, but the symptoms generally last only a few weeks and the patient recovers, often completely."

"Could it be that Lydi has that type?" Anna interrupted, grasping at the hope that her daughter would be able to walk again.

"It is possible, Anna, but we must also face the danger that Lydi may be infected with one or both of the other virus types. These are much more debilitating."

"More debilitating that not being able to move her legs? Barely being able to speak? She could actually get worse?" The last words were spoken in a whisper as the woman stared down at her hands in total devastation.

Dr. Evans' eyes fixed on the road ahead as he drove. He was not sure if this woman who had recently lost her husband could handle any more grief, but he felt that if he was not open with her now, the shock of the disabilities the disease might cause would be far worse to bear. "The second type of polio virus affects the spinal cord. It can cause permanent paralysis of legs and arms." A leaden silence hung over the two as they drove. At last, the man charged on. "The final type of virus affects the brainstem and the muscles needed for breathing and swallowing. With this kind of illness, sometimes an iron lung is needed."

Anna had seen pictures of an iron lung in some of the journals Lydi had brought home from Miss Johnston at school. Her first reaction had been that it looked like a tubular casket. Dreadful images hurtled through her mind. She fervently prayed that her daughter would be spared such misery.

Though he felt like an ogre for giving this woman such an onslaught of details, the physician knew he had to prepare her for the quarantine. "When we get there, Lydi will be taken into the facility and no one will be allowed contact with her. You will need to sign papers and then we have to leave. No good-byes. No hugs."

Anna drew in a deep breath and released it slowly, her eyes brimming with wetness as they swept back to her sleeping child. "How long will it be, Dr. Evans? How long until I can see and hold my child again?"

"The doctors must be certain that she is no longer contagious; then they will administer therapy. It may be several weeks, or more. I know it seems heartless, but the hospital's primary concern must be to keep the polio from spreading."

They rode in silence for the remaining drive while Lydi slept, neither wanting to put their fears into words.

Finally they arrived at Sisters of Mercy Hospital. The mother watched as two nurses hurried to the car, moved Lydi onto a gurney and returned to the doors on the north side of the building. Lydi's eyes fluttered at first, but she seemed blessedly unaware of the situation. Anna entered the office to sign papers, then trudged back to the car, her shoulders heaving with deep sobs. Leaving Lydi that day was the hardest thing she had ever done.

Promises in Courage

CHAPTER 12

ABANDONED

She struggled to open her eyes, for her body had already learned that sleep was the only respite from the pain. As Lydi tried to focus and survey the room, she remembered being carried to Dr. Evans' car to be driven to a hospital. She must have slept through the trip and being transported inside. Nothing looked familiar.

The surroundings were colorless and dull, as though having been scrubbed down to their original surface. The walls and floor were bare and the bed and a table were the only furnishings. There was a space for another patient, but that area was empty.

Something had awakened the girl, though no one else was in the room. The air was heavy with anti-septic and a chemical smell Lydi did not recognize. Where was Dr. Evans? And her mother? Surely they would not have left without telling her good-bye.

Then she heard it. A child's scream of pain. Was it across the hall? "Ouch! You're burnin' me!" There was a snapping sound that reminded Lydi of her mom giving a towel a shake before she hung it on the clothesline. "Oww." The cries diminished to quiet sobs.

Someone spoke sharply, "Hush, girl. Screaming and crying won't make it better."

Lydi longed to jump from her bed and rescue the child, whatever was happening to her. She tried to lift herself in case a miracle had occurred, but her legs still would not move. They felt like logs tied with string to her hips. From her waist down to her toes, Lydi's muscles were useless. The whimpers across the hall gradually subsided, but loneliness and fear began seeping into her, threatening to overtake her very being. She had read stories of children with polio and how debilitating the disease could be. What if she never walked again? Would she spend the rest of her life lying in this hospital bed? Would the paralysis eventually control her entire body? Would she die here in this dreadful place?

Dreams shattered. Hopes and promises dwindled like sand in an hourglass. She pulled the threadbare grayish-white sheet up under her chin and closed her eyes. Silent tears fell to the flimsy pillow until she again succumbed to the solace of sleep.

Promises in Courage

CHAPTER 13

THE DARK SHADOW

A shadow blocked the light from the only window in her room. Though her eyes were shut, Lydi was suddenly aware that something was leaning over her, something big. Cautiously, she squinted her eyes open just a tiny slit, fearful of what might be lurking in this forsaken place.

"Good. You are awake. It's about time." Lydi's eyes opened wide at the person before her, and though she had been taught good manners, she could not help but stare. She had never seen such a large woman before, not just tall, but also very stout. Dressed all in white, she seemed to fill the room. Nurse Leany was printed on her nametag. Lydi's eyes traveled up to the nurse's cap, bobby-pinned to the top of her massive head. The hat seemed so small resting atop the extremely large head, that it reminded the young girl of one her grandmother's frosted vanilla cupcakes.

"You might as well get used to me, Miss Andersson. You can tell I don't put up with lollygagging. One advantage of being a bit plump." She cackled at her own comment, and even her laughter spanned the small room. "Now, I need to take your temperature. Then we'll see if your legs are still paralyzed." She pushed a thermometer in Lydi's mouth as she looked back down at the chart.

"Once the paralysis stops spreading and your temperature drops a bit we begin treatments. You won't like them. They cause pain." Was that a slight smirk that crossed the giant's face, or was it just Lydi's imagination? The woman read the thermometer. "Well, you've still got a pretty high fever." She lumbered out the door and returned a few minutes later with a tiny cup of pills and a glass of water. Sliding one hand under Lydi's back, she lifted her up. Still supporting with her left hand, she poured the pills in the girl's mouth with her right and then held the glass. "You swallow those pills and then drink. You need liquids to fight the fever."

The nurse spoke as she turned to leave. "I'll get you some applesauce and more water. You have to eat, though you probably won't get better. There's no cure for polio, you know. Be sure and holler if you can't breathe or swallow. That means the polio is attacking the muscles that make your lungs work. Then we put you in an iron lung." She chatted as though such an event was a minor, everyday occurrence.

At last, Lydi had a chance to speak, though her voice was hoarse and muted in the tiny space remaining in the room. "There is no need to bring food. I am not hungry."

The looming mass of white sailed back to her bed. "You feeling sorry for yourself, girl? Well, don't. You have it a lot better than some of the kids who come in here. Least you can still use your hands. NOW, as I said before, I'm going to bring you food and you are going to EAT it!"

Lydi's head was turned away, for she refused to let the tyrant see her tears as the bedside tray was left next to her. Finally, when she knew she was alone again, she turned to see a bowl of applesauce and another of Jello cubes. Heaving a great sigh, she tried to reach for the spoon. Her heart pounded wildly and, totally devastated, the young girl stifled a scream. She could no longer move her right hand!

Promises in Courage

CHAPTER 14

OVINE EMPATHY

Michael's heart hurt. Mom had explained to him about polio and the need for Lydi's isolation to keep the disease from spreading. How there could be paralysis, or worse. The boy could not bear to hear any more. He raced out of the house and all the way to the barn. He hauled open the gate on Dottie's pen, ran inside and threw his arms around his beloved black sheep.

"Oh, Dottie, what are we gonna do? Lydi's really sick. Mom said she has to stay in the hospital a long time, and we can't go see her because we could get sick from her." On his knees, the young boy clung to the animal while she stood, listening to her master. He sniffled and went on. "She couldn't even walk to Doc Evans' car yesterday. What if she never walks again? What if she dies?" A soft bleating sound emanated from deep in the sheep's throat, and she rubbed her head against the child's neck as violent sobs racked his body.

He straightened and ran his shirtsleeve under his nose, and with both hands on her head, he looked in Dottie's eyes. "We gotta say prayers, girl, that God will make her better. She just can't die." He shook his head and looked down again, another wave of tears threatening. At that moment the wooly creature began nibbling Michael's hair. He pulled away and smiled through watery eyes.

"I know, Dottie! We'll make her a present! I'll carve something neat out of wood this time. That'll make her happy, and when you're happy, you get better faster. Thanks, girl, I've gotta go to school." He hugged the animal one more time, pulled the gate shut on her pen and then trudged back to the house.

Promises in Courage

CHAPTER 15

MICHAEL HAD A LITTLE LAMB

The other students were filing into the one-room schoolhouse when Anna's pickup pulled into the school yard. She reached over and wrapped Michael in a quick hug. "I love you, Son. See you tonight."

Avoiding his mother's eyes for fear of more tears for both of them, he pushed open the door, jumped out and murmured, "Love you, too, Mom."

The young boy slipped into his desk and went through the motions of the beginning activities of the school day, the Pledge of Allegiance, the song, "My Country Tis of Thee," and Miss Johnston's lesson plans. His thoughts kept drifting back to his sister and what she must be going through all by herself at that hospital.

All at once there was a clattering sound out on the steps and then a *THUMP, THUMP, THUMP* against the front door. Startled at the unusual noise, Miss Johnston walked to the front door hesitantly. There was a commotion among the youngsters as they waited for their teacher to return to the classroom.

"There is a rather large black sheep standing on the front steps," the teacher addressed Michael. Though she was not happy with the interruption, the teacher was fascinated with the special gift the boy seemed to have with animals.

Michael slapped his hand to his forehead and rolled his eyes upward, "Dottie! How did she get out?"

A hubbub of giggles and tittering spread through the classroom, for it was not every day a sheep visited. Emma's hand shot up. "May we please go see Dottie, Miss Johnston? Michael has trained her SO well." Adoration was obvious as she gazed at Michael with a wide smile. Embarrassed at the attention from Emma, Michael squirmed in his seat, but when the teacher asked if he wanted to instruct the others more about his sheep, the boy proudly assented. "Sure, we can go out and see her."

Michael's report about Dorset sheep a year ago had entertained the students and the parents at the open house. When he brought a new baby lamb for the Christmas Program, it was the biggest hit ever. Today everyone was chattering excitedly as they filed outside. The boy hugged his sheep and forgot to scold her for coming to school as the children gathered around him. "This is Dottie. She is the first sheep I got for my flock. She had a lamb, Star, that you all know." Nods and smiles assured Michael that his audience was happily listening. "Sometimes a black sheep is born to a white mother, but it does not happen very often. And Star is white, like her father. Dorset sheep are different from some other sheep because they can have babies pretty much any time of the year." Emma, who had situated herself directly in front of the boy and his sheep, sighed a meaningful sigh. Michael just shook his head and looked to Miss Johnston for help.

The teacher smiled. "Is there anything new you have learned about raising sheep, Michael? Anything you would like to share with the class?"

He thought for a moment, then his face lit up. "Well, yes there is. Dottie is going to have a lamb in the spring. I can tell everybody how that happened." The teacher's mouth dropped open, but Michael did not notice.

"A couple months ago I took Dottie to our neighbors' place, William and Geoffrey's. They have a really big boy sheep. He is called a buck. So Dottie went to stay in their pasture so she could be with the boy sheep, the daddy. Anyway, they….."

"OH, yes, Michael, that talk was very….umm, interesting!" Breathless, Miss Johnston interrupted in the nick of time. "Well, class, thank Michael for the lesson." She spoke "lesson" as if it was a question. "Let's get back inside and continue our classes." She hurried up the steps and motioned for the students to file in. "Michael, do you need to take Dottie home now, or will she be all right until the noon recess?"

"Aw, she'll be fine if I tell her to just wait out here. I think she was worried about me."

"Well, you just talk to your sheep then, and I'll go in and begin our studies." The young teacher shook her head as she walked through the entry room. *I can't believe I just told my student to talk to his sheep!*

Promises in Courage

CHAPTER 16

A SMALL RAY OF LIGHT

The darkness of the early morning hovered over her like a death shroud as Lydi lay in her hospital bed, waiting, pondering. The polio had robbed her body of movement everywhere except her head and her left arm. She remembered Michael's comment that he would rather die than be unable to care for his animals. Now she understood.

The heavy pall descended over the young girl like a demon, slinking in, plunging its claws into her heart, squeezing out every last ounce of hope, every shred of dream that she had ever had. She felt herself fall deeper into the darkness. She longed for her mother to hold her, but she was totally alone. No tears were left to flow, but her body convulsed in uncontrollable sobs.

There was a gentle knock on her door and a glint of light entered the room. "Lydi?" The voice was gentle and soft. "Lydi, Dearie, are you awake?" In the dim light the girl's eyes met those of the stranger, but she did not answer. The young woman sat on the bed and laid her warm hand on Lydi's. "I'm Fiona." She smiled, then added, "Nurse. Cook. Friend. I am here to help you get better."

The light had been extinguished from Lydi's eyes and she simply stared at the ceiling. With a silent prayer, the woman squeezed the girl's hand. "You haven't given up now, have you, girl?"

At last the child slowly turned her head to meet the kind eyes. "What hope is there? I cannot walk, or even move my legs, and last night I lost movement in my hand. What kind of life can I ever have?"

"Ah, girl, the paralysis must be very frightening, but it is not necessarily permanent. We have therapy that we do here, and you may regain the use of those legs. A lot depends on you, though."

A tiny ray of light trickled into Lydi's heart, and the clutch of the demon loosened just a little. Fiona stood. "May I open your shade and allow a bit of light for us?" Lydi nodded and brightness filled the room. "I've made some breakfast for you, Dearie. I'll be back in two jerks of a lamb's tail."

The adage reminded Lydi of Michael and Star and Dottie. She wondered how things were at home, how Mom was doing. Suddenly she felt ashamed that she had not considered what her family was going through. They had to be terribly worried.

Fiona bustled back into the room pushing a bed tray. "We've got scrambled eggs and toast and a huge glass of orange juice." She helped Lydi sit up, arranging the tray in front of her. Lydi was amazed that she actually felt hungry. The nurse, with her white bonnet covering her red curls, hurried out of the room and then returned with a metal chair. "Now, you see what you can do yourself with that hand that works, and I am here to help if you need me."

While Lydi struggled to get the food to her mouth with her left hand, Fiona sat back and talked as though eggs dropped on the sheet and spilled juice was no problem whatsoever. "The Sisters of Mercy started this place for polio patients. They are very dedicated. Every morning in the wee hours the nuns enter each room and say prayers. They help with some of the treatments, but lately they have been working with three youngsters in iron lungs." At the image of the iron lung machines, Lydi's throat constricted and she feared her toast would stick.

Perceiving the girl's anxiety, the nurse added, "Not all polio patients need the iron lung. That is a different polio virus that weakens the breathing muscles. Even those patients can recover and lead a normal life." She watched as Lydi swallowed then attempted another sip of juice. "Dr. Heisze will be in later. He specializes in treating paralytic polio. His ideas deviate somewhat from the traditional methods, but he is more successful. I think you will like him."

The lilting voice sang on, like a birdsong at twilight. As the nurse picked up the stray crumbs, she patted her young patient's arm. "You did just fine, Lydi."

Alone again in the room, Lydi tried to remember what she had read about polio. There was no cure. She recalled that. But there were treatments and exercises that sometimes helped restore movement. Did she dare hope?

Promises in Courage

CHAPTER 17

DR. HEISZE

Someone was whistling. What *was* that tune? "You are My Sunshine." Dad had whistled that melody while they walked, her hand in his. Every Sunday when she was a little girl, she skipped along with him to the corner grocer to buy the *Chicago Tribune.* "I must be dreaming," Lydi thought and let the pleasant memory wash over her.

Her eyes flew open as she heard someone very near clear his throat. "Hello, Miss Lydi Andersson," the tall man said with a warm smile. "I am Dr. Heisze." His gold-flecked eyes sparkled brightly, inviting attention much like the bright green tie that peeked above his lab coat. Dark hair was combed to the side neatly, though William would have hinted that a trim was in order. The energy that radiated from this young man indicated that he had no time for anything as trivial as a haircut.

Lydi extended her left hand shyly. Already she liked this person, though they had just met. "Pleased to meet you, doctor." He clasped her hand with both of his.

"That's the way, girl. Now, tell me all about how you got sick."

She related to the doctor how her legs would not work when she tried to use the treadle, then how she woke up on the davenport and could not move them. How Mom and Dr. Evans had brought her here. "And your other hand?" He spoke softly, almost in a whisper.

"That one worked until last night," Lydi sighed heavily, exasperation in her voice. He nodded, as if affirming something in his mind, then jotted a note on his clipboard.

"You are 12 years old. You live on a farm near your grandparents. You have a mother who loves you, and a little brother. Tell me about your hopes and life plans, Lydi."

Strangely, she felt entirely comfortable talking to this man. She told him of her dream of becoming a doctor, and how she had decided that when her Dad died. How she read journals and texts about medicine. How she had helped Dr. Evans with his office calls last summer. How her friends and family encouraged her not to give up. She stopped talking suddenly and turned away, eyes staring down at her legs.

Dr. Heisze kept smiling. He nodded, and waited, expectantly. "Don't stop, Lydi. I want to hear more."

"More? Look at me! I cannot walk. I cannot even move my legs or feet. I could never be a doctor. How could I get to my patients?" She scooped up her right hand in her left and let it fall like a bag of rice. "How could I operate? Or even administer a shot?"

There was empathy in his eyes as he moved his chair closer. Lydi had a feeling he understood exactly the pain and frustration she was experiencing. He spoke quietly, but with a conviction that shouted certainty. "I am a pediatrician. I have studied and worked with children with polio since..." He hesitated and looked down, then his eyes came back to address his patient. "...for a long time. My theories differ from many other doctors, but what I see here each day reinforces my beliefs. I see children come in with some paralysis, but as they agonize in pain and loneliness, they give up, and when their heart has lost the desire to fight, the virus moves in farther, getting more control."

Lydi's thoughts flashed back to the night she came to the hospital, how helpless and utterly devastated she had felt. That was when she lost movement of her arm.

"Dear child, we are taught that there is no 'cure' for polio, though just what does it mean to be cured? Here at this hospital we administer treatments of moist heat. We do therapy that will help you stretch and use those muscles. You are young and have not been paralyzed long. The road ahead will not be easy. There will be pain, but you can get better."

Lydi swallowed and there were tears in her eyes as she regarded this man who was allowing her to hope.

"It will take courage, Lydi, but I think you have it. I believe that you will walk again, and I want to see you when you do."

No words would come from her throat, which was constricted with emotion. She watched as the doctor stood, moved the chair away from her bed and headed for the door. Was it her imagination, or did Dr. Heisze walk with a limp?

Promises in Courage

CHAPTER 18

THE HOME FRONT

"Do you think she can walk yet? When's she coming home?" Michael questioned his mother, as they sat around the dining room table with Grandma, William and Geoffrey, who stopped in after supper to inquire about Lydi.

Anna tried to smile at her son, but it was impossible to mask the worry in her eyes. "These things may take a while, Michael. She has only been at the hospital for a short time." She passed saucers with cups of Earl Grey to their guests.

"We must go visit her. She needs to know her family cares about her." William's eyes glowed with conviction. He had been particularly upset when Lydi had to be taken to the polio facility.

Anna's hands encircled her tea cup as she spoke quietly, for she had wrestled with the same thoughts as William, but felt helpless to do anything. "We would not be allowed to visit her, William. I am sure of that."

"But I am willing to risk contracting the disease. I would do anything for Lydi. They surely cannot deny us the right to see her when we know the risks."

"Oh, William, I am afraid they can. The disease is highly contagious. I have thought the same as you, that I would risk getting it if I could help my child. But think about it. Do we want to put Michael at risk? His life? His future? Then I think of other mothers. William, I would not wish any other family to endure the agony we are going through. There are many things to consider." Anna looked imploringly at this man—neighbor, friend, now married to her mother, praying he would understand.

Silence reigned for a time with each in their own thoughts. At last Geoffrey spoke. "I have been investigating the disease, the symptoms and the treatments that are being implemented. An Australian woman who was a nurse in the Great War, has had success with moist heat and then therapy to re-strengthen the muscles. I wonder if this specialized facility uses any of these methods." He glanced at his brother. The men could often read each other's thoughts.

Light shone in William's eyes as he comprehended Geoffrey's intentions. "Of course, Brother Geoffrey! I commend your intention. We could bring her home. WE could administer similar treatments."

"Indubitably." Geoffrey replied with a satisfied grin.

William stood resolutely. "Tomorrow Geoffrey and I will go to the hospital. If we are not allowed to see Lydi we will speak with her doctor.

Anna's eyes met her mother's. Anna was doubtful that the two men would accomplish their mission, but somehow, she felt better. At least they would be trying to help. She nodded her assent to William. "I want to send a note to Lydi. Even if you are not allowed to see her, the nurses should be able to give her something from her mother."

"I want her to have this." Michael held up a small kitten he had been whittling. The animal was sleeping with its tail curled in front of its face. The cat was his first attempt at carving an animal other than a sheep. William had taught the boy to carve chunks of pine. The child's mother's eyes filled with tears, for she knew Lydi would treasure her brother's gift.

Christina went to stand next to her husband. "I also wish to send Lydi a token of our love. I will finish it tonight."

"Then we have a plan for tomorrow." Ideas were churning in the man's mind. "It will be of utmost importance that we make a good impression on the individuals who operate the polio facility, espe-cially the doctor. Geoffrey, we will don our suits." William rubbed his whiskered chin, then turned to his wife. "If you have the time, my dear, I believe I am in dire need of a haircut."

Christina nodded tenderly.

Geoffrey turned his head down with a grin and rubbed his hands together in anticipation.

Promises in Courage

CHAPTER 19

HEAT TREATMENT

A loud thump on the door, followed by the sudden harsh glare from the overhead light, jolted Lydi from sleep. "Wakey, wakey! Rise and shine!" A grating voice crushed the silence of the hospital room. There was a rumble of rolling wheels as Nurse Leany swept in, pushing a bed. From beneath the dull sheet, a small head peeked, while two horribly thin arms poked out like sticks holding down the thin fabric at her sides. As the bed trundled by Lydi, her eyes met those of a young girl she guessed to be about Michael's age. Her unruly hair covered part of her face, but she made no attempt to move it. The child looked utterly terrified.

The woman paused for a few moments to catch her breath. Still puffing, she shuffled to Lydi's side. "This is Samantha. She will be your roommate. Well, she will until she has to be put in an iron lung."

Lydi's eyes flew to the child, but Samantha's face was turned to the ceiling. Her eyes were scrunched shut, and a tear was squeezing out, about to meet her matted pillow.

With hands on her ample hips, Nurse Leany announced cheerfully, "Samantha gets to have the first heat treatment today. That way Lydi will see how it is done. Won't that be nice? I'll just go get the hot water." As she waddled out the door, she was humming a tune that sounded like "Over the Rainbow."

"Sorry," Samantha sniffed faintly. "Guess I should try and be brave, but I hate those treatments so bad." She glanced over at Lydi, whose eyes radiated sympathy. "The first time I screamed.

Begged 'em to stop, it hurt so. It felt like it was burning holes in my skin. I still complain plenty."

"The therapy must be terribly painful. How often do we have it?" Lydi asked as she considered that her time would also be coming.

"Sometimes twice a day. I think Nurse Leany likes to make us hurt." A tiny smirk turned up the little girl's mouth as she said, "Sometimes, real quiet-like, so she can't hear, I call her 'Nurse Meany.'" There was a loud racket approaching in the hall. "Oh, no, here she comes!" Dread instantly replaced the smidgen of mirth on the child's face.

Lydi remembered her conversation with Dr. Heisze, how fear and devastation allowed the polio to invade more of the body. "Samantha," Lydi whispered suddenly. "while she is doing the treatment, you can make up a rhyme about her. Just think of silly words to put together." The girl looked doubtful as Nurse Leany clambered in with a cart containing a large steaming pot and a stack of fabric.

The massive woman in white pulled back the flimsy sheet. "Well, Miss Samantha, are we ready for this? You really don't need to be quite so dramatic with your screams and groans. It can't be that bad. You need to be thankful, you know. You are far better off than some of the children who come in here." As she spoke she turned the emaciated, trembling child onto her stomach and lifted the hospital gown to bare her back.

Lydi breathed a silent prayer as she regarded the girl's face. She did not want to watch, but she could not force herself to turn away. For just a second, Samantha opened her scrunched eyes. Lydi tried to nod, to somehow send her the strength to be brave.

At the cart, Nurse Leany counted three layers of the fabric which looked like a wool blanket that had been cut into perfect squares. With thick rubber gloves, she immersed the wool pads into the hot water, then lifted them and squeezed out the water. Working quickly, she flapped them open and plunged them onto the small patient's shoulders, causing her body to jerk at the jolt of sudden heat. But she made no sound except for a rapid intake of breath. The woman frowned, for the child had never taken the heat without painful outbursts. Possibly the water was not hot enough. She slipped off her right glove and stuck her finger into the water. "Ouch!" she hissed, pulling her finger out rapidly and shaking it. Her suspicious glare cut to Lydi, who tried to shrug and look back with innocent puppy eyes.

The hulking figure made a "Humph" sound and stormed out of the room.

Samantha peeked over at Lydi, her voice barely audible. "Nurse Leany is a meany. She likes to make us wail. She is so very big. Her dress must be a sail."

Promises in Courage

CHAPTER 20

SAMANTHA'S STORY

The rumble of large wheels turning echoed down the hall as it drew closer to the girls' room. Samantha shuddered. "That's the iron lung thing. They're bringing it here for me." She spoke quietly, resigned to her fate.

Lydi studied the girl next to her, wishing fervently that she could convey some kind of hope. "But the iron lung is to help you breathe. You look to me like you are breathing fine."

"Well, actually, my throat just started hurting," Samantha swallowed hard, fear constricting her throat. "It doesn't matter anyway. I don't have anything to get better for."

"You mean you don't have a family?" Lydi questioned gently, worried that she was inflicting more pain on the child.

"Yeah, I've got a family, but they won't be able to take care of me. I've got three sisters and two little brothers, one's just a baby. No way can my mom take care of a cripple."

"I am sure they love you, Samantha, and will help you every way they can." Lydi thought of her own family and the measures she knew they would take to make her life better.

"I s'pose they love me, but love don't put food on the table. Pa almost lost the farm when I was little. I remember being really hungry every night when we went to bed. Then it started rainin' again and he got a crop. But, eight people take a lot of work. Ma's about run ragged. She don't need to be saddled waitin' on me."

Lydi's heart hurt for the child, feeling her staggering hopelessness. "They'll figure out a way to manage; that is what families do."

"Nah, not if they can't. I heard Aunt Frieda tell Ma that I could just go to an orphanage. The county 'll take care o' me." Tears flooded Samantha's eyes and she looked away and choked out, "I'd just as soon die."

Just then a loud male voice boomed right outside their door. "WHAT IS THIS MACHINE DOING HERE?" Someone uttered a response in the background, but Lydi could not decipher the words. Suddenly they heard a clank, followed by the clamor of rolling wheels receding back down the hall.

Seconds later Dr. Heisze strode into the room. His eyes quickly took in each of the girls, then he flashed a bright smile. "How are my two favorite patients doing today?" Neither replied, for thoughts of the iron lung hovered over them, a shadow of gloom. The man rubbed his chin in thought. "Hmmm. Well, I hope neither of you have anything on your social calendars for this afternoon. We are going to be busy for a while."

Promises in Courage

CHAPTER 21

THE FOUR MUSKETEERS

Nurse Fiona maneuvered the cart of heat therapy devices through the door. Seconds later Dr. Heisze marched into the room, clipboard in hand. He drew in a deep breath, and with determination in his voice, the young doctor outlined his plan of action.

Samantha was to have the hot compresses reapplied by the nurse; then the doctor would assist her with exercises to strengthen her muscles. Lydi would then follow the same course of treatments with the purpose of fighting the paralysis.

Fiona gently pressed the hot moist pads against the small child's shoulders, working down her back, then on to her knees, legs and feet. Samantha closed her eyes, not uttering a sound as the heat penetrated through her body. At last the girl spoke. "I'm sure glad I've got you puttin' on those hot-packs, 'stead of Nurse Leany. Don't hurt as bad when you do it."

The doctor glanced up from his chart, wanting to add his own thoughts of Nurse Leany at the moment, wondering how his nurse would reply.

Fiona massaged Samantha's legs through the wet fabric, considering her response. "Well, Dearie, Nurse Leany has worked here for several years. Maybe she has seen some things that made her sad. I think she copes with that melancholy by pretending she is happy."

"I don't know," replied Samantha thoughtfully. "I still think she's mean."

"It might seem like she doesn't care," the nurse spoke as she rubbed around the girl's ankles. "Do you think maybe she acts all cheerful and carefree so she doesn't feel sad for the patients?"

Dr. Heisze cleared his throat. "It is my turn to work with Samantha. Nurse Fiona, if you will now please apply the moist heat to our patient, Lydi?"

He moved to the child's bedside, adjusted the hospital gown to cover her, and gently turned her to her back. Then he raised the bed closer to sitting position, watching her face for signs of pain. Speaking in reassuring tones, he began to manipulate her feet, gently pulling and turning, just small movements at a time. Finally she winced in pain and he shifted to her knees.

Mournful eyes met those of the kind doctor and at last Samantha murmured, "Don't know why you're workin' so hard. Won't do any good."

"Well, young lady, I beg to differ on that. Physical therapy can do a world of good. If you build up these muscles, you will walk again."

A ray of hope lit in the child's eyes. "Ya think I can ever really, truly walk? Just like I used to?"

"I do," replied the doctor with certainty in his voice. "But, Sammy, you will have to work on it."

A hint of smile twitched on the girl's lips. "That's what my pa calls me, 'Sammy.'"

"Well, then, let's get to work so you can go home and your pa can have his Sammy back again. Muscles get strong when you use them. Do you think you can do exercises if I show you how?"

"I think so," she replied hesitantly and waited quietly for a few seconds. "Will ya show me, please, Doc?"

Promises in Courage

CHAPTER 22

HOPE?

"Lydi Andersson, you might even take over my medical practice someday." Dr. Heisze looked directly into his patient's eyes as his hands deftly massaged and stretched her right shoulder. Doubt clouded the girl's face, but as the young physician continued the therapy, he explained.

"The polio virus has affected the part of your brain that controls the muscles in your arm and legs, thus causing the paralysis. Muscles need to move or they become weak. The longer they are immobile, the more difficult it becomes to move them again. The moist heat relaxes the muscles, allowing easier movement. It is up to you to get them moving again."

He had worked all the way down her shoulder, elbow and wrist. "Even a slight movement is progress. Small steps. Now, Lydi, try to move your fingers."

She had only known this man for a short time, but he emanated a sense of caring and assurance which inspired trust. Could she someday inspire her own patients in the same way? A tiny ember of hope warmed her heart. With a deep breath, she willed her fingers to move.

Promises in Courage

CHAPTER 23

VOICES

Lydi awoke and peered about the hospital room. She must have been dreaming, for she had heard voices. Loud voices. One was Dr. Heisze, and she was certain the other booming outburst was William. Quiet Grandpa William? Uncontrolled anger was so uncharacteristic of the man; Lydi dismissed the voices as a meaningless fantasy.

"Silent Night" was playing softly somewhere down the hall. A pang stung Lydi's heart as she realized she would not be home for Christmas. All the exciting plans she had made with Mom and Grandma had been futile. She felt herself slipping back into gloom as she thought of the times missed, the baking, making and hiding the presents. She longed for her family. She wanted to go home.

A woman in a dark skirt and white blouse hastened into the room, her arms piled high with various items. She carefully set them down on the bed next to Lydi and beamed. "I have a delivery for you, Miss Andersson." She placed a tiny Christmas tree on the bed stand. Under the tree she tucked a stack of books. Lydi recognized them as her favorites from home. On top of the books was an envelope addressed to the girl in her mother's handwriting. The lady then laid a tiny carved kitten on the envelope. Finally, she unfolded a small quilt and spread it gently over Lydi's arms. "Someone obviously loves you a lot and wants you to get better soon." She gently patted Lydi's shoulder and retreated to the door.

Minutes later, Dr. Heisze strode in and greeted both girls. "How are we doing today, Sammy? Lydi? I see you have already received the items that were delivered this morning, Lydi. Your grandfather is a determined, tenacious man. Also, extremely obstinate."

Confused for a few seconds, Lydi stared at the doctor, open mouthed.

"I like him. He reminds me of me." Chuckling softly, the doctor marched out of the room.

Promises in Courage

CHAPTER 24

CHAPTER 24

CLOSE ENCOUNTERS

The brim of the black cloche hat cast a shadow over her eyes. Not a hair escaped the wool covering to soften her severe features, the small pointed nose, strong cheek bones and jutting chin. She sat rigidly on the metal bench, eyes focused on the snow-packed street ahead of them, gloved hands clutching the handles of her plain leather purse, which held all the money they would need for their bus and train tickets. If Billie had not known the woman sitting next to her to be patient and kind, she surely would have been intimidated by her for-midable appearance. Small featherlike flakes coated their hats, and floated down to Billie's hand-knitted blue mittens, an early Christmas present from her sister, Drucilla.

"How late do you think the bus will be, Miss Nelson?" Billie watched a beat-up brown truck crawl slowly by on the road as the snowy sky darkened into evening. "The ride to Gunnison may take several hours in this weather."

The teacher's features softened as she felt the excitement of the young girl next to her. "We will make it in time for the five AM train to Denver, Billie, barring some dire fate." A slight frown crossed her eyes as though she was remembering something. She turned to her traveling companion and changed the subject. "I imagine your cousin, Ethel, is as excited as you are. I hope you have an enjoyable visit in Iowa. You will have much to talk about."

Billie sat upright with anticipation. "Oh, yes! My cousin, Esther, will be there, too. She is already a teacher like Ethel wants to be. Tomorrow night is the school Christmas program, and I will finally get to meet Ethel's classmates. Do you remember me telling you about Lydi? She has written several letters to me and I consider her my dear friend. Do you think you can be true friends with someone you have never met?"

Miss Nelson nodded slightly and Billie chattered on. "Ethel said we are invited to tea at Lydi's grandma's house." A small puff of snow sparkled in the air as Billie's mittens clasped together. "Thank you, Miss Nelson, for inviting me to travel to Iowa with you, and for buying my train ticket." Billie remembered the dollar bills that were tucked in her boot, a dollar her father had given her, and the other she had been saving for a special occasion. There was one dime left in her piggy bank, what was left from what she and Dru had earned washing windows and pounding the coal dust out of rugs for their neighbor. Billie had taken the remaining dimes and nickels to the company store to exchange for a dollar bill.

The woman reached over to pat Billie's hand. "As I told your father, it is a favor to me to have a traveling companion. I will not ride the rails alone, ever again." Her face clouded as she stared down at the whiteness on the walk for a few seconds. "Since I moved to Baldwin to teach at the mining camp, I have missed my sister, Clara, immensely. Were it not for you, I would be unable to spend an early Christmas with family. I also thank you, Billie."

A long, gray vehicle turned the corner to the station and Billie thrilled at the sound of the approaching bus wheels plowing through snow.

The driver announced the next cities on his route. When he called, "Gunnison," they were the first passengers to ascend the three battered steps. Miss Nelson gently nudged Billie's elbow, indicating that they were to take the seat directly behind the driver, with Billie next to the window. A young couple followed them, settling two seats back on the opposite side, brushing snow from their thin, worn coats. The woman carried a bundle wrapped in a soft warm blanket. She folded back part of the blanket to form a small hole. As the mother peeked in, Billie could hear soft cooing. She looked down at her own coat, a hand-me-down from Dru, and felt a rush of thankfulness.

An older gentleman climbed onto the bus, removed his bowler hat as he nodded greetings to the driver and Miss Nelson, and found a seat near the middle of the bus. In an uproar of wild laughter three young men clamored in and headed to the back seats. Billie felt Miss Nelson's body tense and lean unconsciously toward her. She clutched her purse tightly as they passed.

"Everybody ready?" the driver asked as he glanced up into his mirror at the passengers, closed the folding door and shifted into drive. The baby fussed for a few minutes, but soon quieted with the motion of the bus. Miss Nelson stared ahead into the oncoming snow. Billie surveyed the scenes as they rolled by in the ensuing darkness. Red and green lights glowed from storefronts as the bus creeped through Baldwin. At last, contented with the spirit of Christmas, the girl laid her head back on the seat.

A train whistle blared nearby and Billie was jolted awake. "We have arrived in Gunnison, Billie. I am glad you were able to sleep." A glance at her teacher confirmed that Miss Nelson had not experienced the same luxury.

The train station was well-lit in the wee hours of the morning, and in contrast with the quiet bus depot, bustled with activity. Passengers were arriving for the ride to Denver and eventually to the east coast on the Rio Grande Railroad. The ticket clerk assigned cars as the travelers gathered at the counter. After handling the ticket transaction, Miss Nelson led Billie to a shiny oak bench near the door. Billie wondered why the woman had not chosen a quieter spot near the back. Her eyes darted back and forth nervously, searching the faces of each person who approached them.

Time flew quickly as they watched more people enter the station. "All aboard the train to Denver!" the conductor called as he poked his head in the door, then disappeared in the darkness. Miss Nelson nearly jumped up at the announcement. She grabbed her bag and Billie followed. They were the first passengers to board the car bound for Iowa and Nebraska. Again, the older woman indicated where Billie was to sit and, with a sigh of relief, settled down next to her.

"I have found that certain seats are safer..." She paused for a moment and then forced a smile, "I mean--more pleasant for the journey. We want to be close to the conductor and far away from the men's 'facility.'" She shuddered as she glanced back at the men's restroom. Billie studied her teacher for a few moments. She was obviously nervous about something. Was it just traveling, or had something happened in the past? Something that made her fear every male who set foot upon a bus or train? Billie began to understand why they had endured sitting at the front of the train depot. The woman felt safer when they were in plain sight.

In less than ten minutes the whistle pierced the air and the car lurched forward. Most of the other passengers had stored their bags and sat anticipating the ride. Suddenly, from the back of the train a man floundered up the aisle, singing a rather lewd melody Billie had never heard. "'Scuze me, mmmadam," he hiccupped as he brushed against a woman who humphed in disgust at the drunken man. As he neared their seats, Billie saw Miss Nelson's knuckles grow white, clutching her purse even tighter. Chin held high she stared ahead, willing the man to walk by. "Hmmm, an' what have we here?" He tried to doff his hat with a flourish, but ended up dropping it in the aisle just at the teacher's feet. Spit flew as he stammered. "Two little purties. I think I will just sit...." He reached down for his hat just as the engine picked up speed and fell directly over Miss Nelson with his head on Billie's lap.

"You get off that girl, you big oaf!" Abruptly the purse was transformed to a weapon that pelted the man's back and head relentlessly. "Oh! The! Nerve!" Each word was punctuated with another purse blow.

The conductor hastened up the aisle from somewhere in the back. He grabbed the befuddled man by the shoulders of his coat, removed him from Miss Nelson's reach and roughly escorted him to the rear of the train.

"Are you all right, Billie?" She reached for the girl's hand in concern, then released a great sigh as Billie nodded. "I am so grateful the conductor came when he did to rescue us." She pushed a strand of hair back under her hat that had escaped in the fracas, then sniffed and straightened her spine.

Billie turned her head to the window, unable to contain a grin. There was no question in her mind as to who was really rescued. From far in the back she heard someone plop onto a seat with a pitiful groan. She wasn't sure, but she thought she heard

him mumble, "Thhhank you, Mmmmister Con-
ducter. You ssssaved my life."

Promises in Courage

CHAPTER 25

THE CHRISTMAS PROGRAM

Little Vicky Christleton's hand covered her mouth as she emitted her characteristic giggle-snort. She and Ricky had just finished their own rendition of "Up on the Housetop," and her brother had dropped the cardboard chimney just as Santa was about to jump down. The audience laughed and applauded as the children scurried off the stage, Ricky to his father, Greg, and Vicky to Ethel's lap in the front row.

Billie was pleased to be in the middle of the girls Ethel and Lydi had written about. Mabel, Julia, and Lilly had welcomed her warmly when Ethel introduced her cousin from Colorado, but she was disappointed that she would not get to meet Lydi.

Her thoughts wandered to the girl, quarantined in the polio ward; how terrified she must be.

Miss Johnston was holding up a jar filled with coins and bills, drawing Billie's thoughts back to the program. "Lydi Andersson is hospitalized at the Sisters of Mercy Polio Facility in Council Bluffs. Right now she is paralyzed from the waist down. Our class has decided to give the money in the donation jar to the Andersson family to help with Lydi's expenses, if they will accept it." Vicky beamed and clapped her hands. "If anyone wishes to add to the jar it will be here at my desk," the teacher added.

The students shuffled to their places in front of the room and began singing "Silent Night." The parents and visitors joined in, no one caring if they sang off-tune. As the crowd neared the final verse, Billie discreetly reached down and slipped off her boot. The throng pushed toward the refreshment table in the entry. Billie slipped her dollar bill into the jar.

Promises in Courage

CHAPTER 26

DOCTOR SHOCK

He stopped short as he entered the hospital room, then stood, transfixed, as he regarded the hopeful sight before him. His two newest polio patients had managed to move their wheelchairs side-by-side. Lydi's right arm was intertwined with Sammy's left arm and together, they were holding a book. Lydi was reading with expression and Sammy was following along with her eyes, totally captivated by the words:

"And how did little Tim behave?" asked Mrs. Cratchit when she had rallied Bob on his credulity and Bob had hugged his daughter to his heart's content.

"As good as gold," said Bob, "and better. Somehow he gets thoughtful, sitting by himself so much, and thinks the strangest things you ever heard. He told me, coming home, that he hoped the people saw him in the church, because he was a cripple, and it might be pleasant to them to remember upon Christmas Day, who made lame beggars walk, and blind men see."

Lydi's eyes had swept to her young friend's face as she read the word "cripple." Sammy just smiled and nodded, an indication that Lydi should keep reading.

Dr. Heisze shook his head in amazement. Weren't these girls confined to bed just yesterday? Did not each of them express total hopelessness for her future? As he watched he saw movement in Sammy's legs. He had no doubt she would continue to recover now. Lydi's right hand bent just a little as the page needed to be turned. Mr. Dickens would surely be pleased knowing his Christmas Carol story was helping two young girls heal each other.

Still undetected, the man quietly backed out of the room, fervently hoping they would have enough time.

Promises in Courage

CHAPTER 27

SCANDINAVIAN DELICACY

Ethel and Billie spread creamy butter over the flat disks of bread on their plates. Grandma set out sugar, honey, jam and syrup, encouraging them to try the different sweets on their lefse. Then they rolled the buttery toppings inside and took a bite.

Billie's eyes sparkled with delight. Her mother made special treats for the holidays, but she had never tasted anything quite like this. "This is wonderful, Grandma Christina!" She felt comfortable addressing the woman as 'Grandma' since reading and re-reading Lydi's letters about her family.

Ethel thought of Lydi, but was afraid to voice her thoughts for fear that the joyful time they were sharing would turn to sadness. She remembered what their friends at school had said when Ethel told them they were having lefse with Lydi's grandmother, and spoke brightly, "Mabel, Lilly and Julia love lefse, too. Their older sister, Ida, helped make some last week. She said she didn't mind peeling the ten pounds of potatoes, but she got tired of rolling out all those big circles."

"It does take some time, and there is a knack to it, as sometimes they get holes or break when we take them to the stove top." Christina smiled. "William helped me bake them and flip them over, though he reminded me several times he prefers crumpets."

"Mabel said it takes hundreds of lefse for their big hungry family." Ethel grinned as she went on, "I guess their mother, Selma, wrapped up five plates and stored them in the pantry so they would have plenty for Christmas. After two days, she noticed that the piles were growing smaller. Someone was stealing the lefse!"

Christina smiled and shook her head. "I would guess it was one of those young boys. Aren't there four brothers, besides the girls?"

"There are," confirmed Ethel, "but turns out the culprit was not one of the boys at all; it was their younger sister, Emma!"

"Can't say as I blame her. These are so good." Billie closed her eyes, savoring the tender rich delicacy.

"Lydi and I had made plans to make lefse together," Christina sighed, and a look of sadness crossed her face. "I do wish she could enjoy time with you girls. She was looking forward to meeting you in person, Billie."

There was a commotion as the back door opened and the women heard male voices. "Did I hear you call us in for tea?" Geoffrey peeked into the dining room door with a smile. "We brought in more cobs and wood for the stove, just in case you ate all the lefse already and we need to make more."

Christina introduced Billie to William and Geoffrey as the gentlemen bowed politely and shook her hand. They pulled up chairs across the dining room table and welcomed the girls warmly to their home. Billie's stories of the mining camps gave them all a greater insight into the kind of life the girl and her family led.

The rest of the afternoon passed quickly in pleasant conversation and disappearing lefse, and inevitably the conversation came back to Lydi. "She was looking forward to meeting you." William stared into his tea. Then he looked up at his brother and Christina could tell that they were silently communicating in their twin way.

"When do you have to return to Colorado, young lass?" Geoffrey addressed Billie.

"I am supposed to meet Miss Nelson at the train station on Friday," Billie frowned. "Esther will need to take me very early so that she won't be late for her teaching job. I don't like imposing, but…" Again, the brothers made eye contact.

"There is no imposition, Billie. We are so happy that you could visit. It will all work out fine." Ethel patted her cousin's hand graciously.

"Thank you so much," replied Billie. "Maybe I can come again soon and meet Lydi then." She knew it was probably not proper to speak her thoughts but she at last blurted out what had been on her mind ever since she knew Lydi had polio. "Where could she have caught the polio virus? How could this have happened to her?"

Geoffrey answered the question that all of Lydi's family had wrangled for days. "It is baffling, is it not, Billie? Polio is highly contagious. It can be spread in many ways, I have read, even through the air or in drinking water. There was an outbreak in Des Moines a few weeks ago, with 63 reported cases. Possibly somehow the virus was transferred from someone there. We will probably never know exactly how Lydi contracted the disease."

Tears pooled in her eyes and her hands clenched, Billie could no longer contain her emotions. "I don't know why Lydi had to get it! She is so kind and thoughtful. It's just not right. I hate polio!"

William reached across the table and gently squeezed the girl's hand. "We understand, Billie, and struggle daily with similar queries, but we have grand hopes for Lydi's recovery."

Each person nodded silently as eyes bent to the table in weighted thought.

After a moment, Geoffrey lifted his head, straightened his spine and spoke with conviction. "Better to light a candle than to curse the darkness."

Promises in Courage

CHAPTER 28

LIGHTING THE CANDLE

"I am quite certain that Lydi's polio virus is no longer contagious," Dr. Heisze spoke quietly to William and Geoffrey, as they all sat around the table in the cramped conference room. "However, for several reasons, I do wish she could remain here a bit longer. She is beginning to recover from the paralysis, and her companionship with…"

"She will continue to recover at home." William interrupted sternly, determined to accomplish the feat that he and Geoffrey had set out to finish. "Possibly more quickly, for she will have the love and support of her family."

"I certainly cannot deny that," the doctor conceded, "and I can no longer insist that you leave her here." He stood then, trying to mask the anguish in his voice, for he had grown close to the young patients who were working so hard to encourage each other. Sammy would miss her friend and possibly regress in her healing process. He had hoped for a little more time.

He firmly grasped each of the brother's hands. "I give you my blessing and hope with all my heart that she will fully recover. I admire your courage." With a solemn nod, he walked out the door.

Nurse Leany clamored into Lydi's hospital room with a large garbage can in tow. She tramped to the table next to Lydi's bed, grabbed a handful of books and began dropping them into the garbage.

"What? What are you DOING?" Lydi cried. "Why are you throwing away my books?"

"Hospital policy. All released patient's belongings must be destroyed to avoid risk of spreading the polio virus." She reached for the precious quilt Grandma had stitched with Michael's carving lovingly resting on top of it.

"Wait!" Lydi's left hand flew out and, unconsciously, her right hand also moved slightly to stop the nurse. "I don't know what is going on, but if I am leaving, then could I please give these things to Sammy? At least she can enjoy them for a while."

"Humph, rules are rules, and I don't see why they should be bent just for the likes of you." She rolled her eyes and turned back to the door. "But, I will ask the doctor." She left muttering something about "his little favorites."

Fiona rushed in, breathless with excitement. "Lydi, you are going home! You will be with your family for Christmas. Let's get you dressed and ready."

A pang of sadness hit Lydi suddenly and she looked over at Sammy. "Oh, Sammy, I wish you could come home with me. I will miss you." The child's mournful eyes spoke volumes and Lydi hoped with all her heart that she would not regress from her miraculous progress the last few days.

"I'm glad for ya, Lydi." Then she looked away for in her heart she did not want her friend to go home.

Fiona gave Sammy a quick hug. "Didn't Nurse Leany tell you? Your pa stopped early this morning. Dr. Heisze told him you are well on your way to recovery and you can go home as soon as you can stand alone. Sammy, you almost did that last night."

"Pa wants me to come home?" A relieved smile mingled with the tears on the child's face.

With an excessive amount of huffing and puffing Nurse Leany marched in, plopped a large stack of books on Sammy's bedside table, then unfolded the quilt with a spiteful slap and laid it on top of the books. "And here is the CAT!" She tossed it carelessly at Sammy and stormed out.

Sammy adeptly caught the small carving. Flashing a smile that lit up Lydi's heart she pushed her legs off the side of the bed and sat. "Thanks, Lydi."

Fiona placed an envelope in Lydi's left hand, then pushed her wheelchair out of the quarantined area into the room where Grandpa William and Geoffrey waited. Hugs and happy tears and a sense of excitement filled the room. The tinsel on the sparsely decorated tree in the corner seemed to stir, emitting a happy sparkle. Covered in a warm quilt Anna had sent, Lydi helped wheel herself to this next step of her journey.

"We have a surprise waiting for you in the car." Geoffrey rubbed his hands together in anticipation.

Forty-five minutes later, Lydi was on her way home, Ethel next to her in the back seat and William and Geoffrey in front. She had gotten to meet Billie at last, though for just a short time as they rode with William to the train station to meet Miss Nelson. Lydi felt an even stronger kinship with her friend. They would meet again, and in the meantime they would write letters. A sting of reality threatened to steal her joy when she thought of her worthless writing hand. With heart and soul she wished her fingers to move as she stared down at her hand. Her thumb. It bent! Her hand shook. Was that movement in the fingers, too?

Suddenly realizing she still held the envelope in her hand, she worked to open it and remove the small slip of paper. It was from Dr. Heisze. "Remember, Lydi, I want to see you walk."

Exhausted, but with a deep sense of hope, Lydi smiled and reached for Ethel's hand. She let her head fall back against the seat and exhaled slowly as the last words she and Sammy had read late last night, Tiny Tim's words, danced back into her head: "A Merry Christmas to us all; God bless us, every one!"

Promises in Courage

CHAPTER 29

HOME FOR CHRISTMAS

Michael literally jumped up from his chair. "I'll get you another lefse, Lydi! Can I help you put on the butter? Just let me roll it up for you." The adults gathered around the dining room table for Christmas dinner smiled indulgently. Michael was thrilled to have his sister home again.

"Thank you, Michael. I think I can do it." Lydi was becoming adept at using her left hand. Her right hand had limited movement, but it worked as an anchor, and she knew from what Dr. Heisze had taught her that she must keep moving her muscles that worked. Tomorrow, heat treatments and therapy would begin at Grandma's house. Grandma,

Grandpa William and Geoffrey had her room prepared. The path ahead would be agonizing. For today, she wanted only to enjoy Christmas with her family and allow herself to hope.

Geoffrey managed to get everyone to laugh at his brother's expense. The two bantered good-naturedly. Grandma shook her head, accustomed to the brothers' antics. Anna surveyed her loved ones, trying with her very soul to feel the spirit of thankfulness. Her gaze rested on her daughter as she struggled with every movement, and the stark reality hit Anna and something twisted in her heart. What lay ahead for their family? Could she deal with the pain of watching her child struggle through such a devastating disability? Would Lydi have the courage to endure?

All thoughts were interrupted by a light knock at the front door. "Who could that be, calling on Christmas Day?" Christina wondered, as Anna stood.

"Sally! Merry Christmas to you." Anna greeted the teacher warmly, but could not help but wonder what brought her to their home on Christmas Day.

"Thank you, Anna, and a Merry Christmas to all of you." She beamed at Lydi, then held up a jar, filled to the brim with coins and bills. "We decided to give our Christmas donation to Lydi to help pay for her stay in the hospital." She held the heavy vessel out to Anna. "If you will accept it?"

Anna looked down at the floor. She remained quiet for a few seconds, then lightly touched the teacher's arm. "Please come in. I think you should present the gift to Lydi yourself."

Lydi wished that she could stand and face her beloved school teacher, but she knew today that was impossible. She looked around the room at each of the people who loved her. Finally, her eyes met her mother's. Dad had been adamant that his family would never accept charity. "We can stand on our own two feet. Pay our own bills," he would often say. Lydi knew her mother felt the same way. Suddenly she knew what she must do.

She reached for the jar with her left hand. Michael stepped in to help set it on the table. "Thank you, Miss Johnston. I know that this money comes from families who have very little, but still they shared." She swallowed hard and took a deep breath. "With your blessing, I would like to give this gift to someone who needs it much more than I. Her name is Sammy."

Anna could not stop the tears that flowed as she went to hug her daughter. William turned to his brother and a look passed between them. William's lips turned up as Geoffrey nodded. They would deliver the money for Sammy to the hospital. "I presume that tomorrow would be a most opportune time to call on the good doctor."

Promises in Courage

CHAPTER 30

A HEAVY BURDEN

3:00 AM. He sat in the cold morning kitchen with his face in his hands. She padded in softly, stood behind him, and laid her hands on his shoulders. Though they had been married only a few months, she knew, instinctively, when he needed her. "What is troubling you, my husband?"

"I apologize for waking you, dear Christina." He rubbed his hands over his unshaven face and shook his head dismally. "I cannot stop worrying about Lydi. She has been with us nearly a month. I practically boasted to Dr. Heisze that she would be walking by now if she were with us. Why is her progress so slow?"

She took both of his hands in hers and looked directly into his eyes. "As you have often said, William, these things take time."

He withdrew his hands from hers, lifted them palms up, and then dropped them back to the table with a thud. "How much time do we have, Christina? Every day that her legs remain sedentary, the muscles atrophy further. What if she never walks again?"

"Healing does not always happen immediately. Besides, the girl has made progress. Her right hand is almost back to normal. She has gained some movement in her left foot. Today she was able to pick up a pencil with her toes. I don't know if I could even do that!"

"But she should be standing, at least. Possibly I should have left her for a longer time at the hospital." His head fell to his chest.

The picture of total devastation tore at his wife's heart. She drew in a deep breath and again reached for his hand. "William, do you think possibly you are forgetting to ask God for help? Sometimes we try to carry the entire load ourselves when we should be asking for guidance from the one who heals."

There was a light knock next to the kitchen door, accompanied by the sound of Geoffrey clearing his throat. He peeked around the corner, then pulled up a chair next to his brother. After a quick glance at the others, Geoffrey rubbed his hands together and flashed a silly grin, obviously in his twin mind-reading mode. "You are discussing the progress of our dear Lydi; Christina is entirely correct in her supposition that we have been far too independent in our endeavors with Lydi's therapy. The girl and Michael and all her friends have been praying for miracles. I suggest that we ask Him to work through us to achieve them. Shall we reconvene this assembly at breakfast?"

Promises in Courage

CHAPTER 31

CHANGE IN STRATEGY

Something tickled her nostrils and roused her from a sound sleep. What was that smell? Christina lay still for a few moments until she heard the cuckoo clock in the hall sing five times. Tying her blue gingham apron over her cotton dress, she found Geoffrey standing in front of the cook stove, a long wooden spoon slowly circling through a steaming hot liquid. A minty smell permeated the air in the kitchen, mixed with a fragrance similar to the one that burst from the pine chunks William split with his ax.

Geoffrey glanced up, a satisfied smile on his face. "The coffee pot is on, dear lady."

"Thank you, Geoffrey." Christina poured herself a cup and set about preparing bacon, eggs, and toast for the brothers, who would soon head to the barn to do the milking.

Suddenly a white-haired gentleman, dressed in red plaid flannel shirt and overalls hurried into the kitchen, adjusting his suspenders over his shoulders. He sniffed the heavy air. "Geoffrey, you have formulated a new concoction! A liniment for Lydi's muscles. A splendid idea!"

Joining in the excitement, Christina's eyes shone. "Can we add an extra heat and massage treatment using your liniment? I can administer that one while you two are doing the milking."

"That is a splendid proposal, dear wife. I also have devised a plan during the night. Sunshine and fresh air may also benefit the child. I don't know why I have felt she needed to be restricted to indoor activity," William chimed in. "Tomorrow we will take her on a stroll outside."

Fragments of the dismal cloud of discouragement floated out the chimney with the smoke from the cook stove, replaced by a new sense of hope and trust.

Geoffrey leaned carefully over the kettle as he continued to stir. He drew in a great whiff of the infused steam. "AAHHH," he breathed out, contentedly. "Heavenly."

Promises in Courage

CHAPTER 32

STRONGER THAN YOU THINK

The golden red orb streamed its iridescent ribbons to earth, tempering the cold morning air. Lydi leaned her head back onto the sturdy wooden chair. She closed her eyes and luxuriated in the light as its heavenly arms reached down, wrapped around her, and renewed her body, warming her very bones. It had been months since she had been outside. William had driven her to the orchard and helped her to his chair, half carrying, half dragging her as she leaned against his side.

The brightness penetrated her eyelids like a meteor shower on a dark night, and she felt a lightness, a renewing sense of strength she had not felt since the polio set in. Nearby, William cleared his throat softly. "Lydi. Are you ready to help me?"

"Oh, of course, Grandpa William. I was just enjoying the sun."

"As you should, my child. It has always been my theory that the sun possesses healing capabilities." He handed her six lengths of twine, each about eight inches long, and three slips of paper. Each paper had a name on it: Wealthy, Jonathan, and Chieftain. "If you would please assist me with tying and labeling the scions that I bring to you, I would be most grateful. Here are six from the Wealthy tree. You may bundle them together and tie at the top and bottom."

"Why are you saving sticks, Grandpa?"

The man smiled gently. "We will use these sticks, or scions, to graft onto new rootstocks that Geoffrey and I have grown, thus producing more apple trees. We need to label them so we know what varieties grow from the successful grafts we do in the spring.

Lydi nodded thoughtfully. "Would it be better just to cut the scions at the same time? They would be fresher."

"One would think so, Lydi, and I understand your questioning, but the scion needs to be dormant, as the fruit trees are through the winter. In spring, the trees will leaf and grow. We cut the small branches from last year's growth, wrap them in a damp cloth and store them under the snow until spring. I hope that you will also assist with the grafting in March and April."

Lydi bound the scions together and then began to tuck the paper labels under the bands. She was glad that her hands were both working again. It felt good to be useful. To enjoy the brisk winter air.

Suddenly a large blob of snow zoomed in and hit her on the shoulder of her dark wool coat. She let out a yelp, startled by the unexpected attack.

"Oh, Lydi, I am so sorry!" Michael shouted from a three-foot snow drift that flanked the orchard next to the road. "I didn't mean to hit you, honest, I didn't. I was aiming for the chair."

Her little brother seemed so remorseful, she almost felt sorry for him, but something about the sunshine, the fresh air and the wonder of moving again amid the trees sprouted a small seed of mischief within the girl. She used her hands to push her body down to the ground, grasped a handful of snow and hurled it at her brother as he ran toward her.

William rested a hand on a low branch of his beloved Jonathan apple and watched. Michael rushed to his sister, his boots losing traction in the wet snow. "Are you all right, Lydi? Why did you fall?"

Just then she flung another clump right into his face. He stopped suddenly, then burst out laughing at his sister's retaliation. She smiled smugly, reached for the chair and managed to climb back in it.

Still at a distance from his newly acquired grandchildren, William's heart pounded with excitement.

Pulling down his hat to cover his eyes and his smile, the gentleman resumed his pruning and listened as the youngsters engaged in cheerful banter. Their laughter was a balm for his soul, and a flame of hope flickered again. Possibly his precious wife had been right.

As he lopped off a branch here and there, preparing the tree for new life in the spring, he wondered if Lydi even realized she had moved her legs when she crawled into the chair. Sunshine and fresh air is already working to diminish the paralysis, he thought. *I am so glad the idea came to me!*

Promises in Courage

CHAPTER 33

ETHEL'S VISIT

Ethel hurried down the lane in the afternoon sun, her arms laden with books and papers. Seeing her good friend waiting for her in one of the rocking chairs, she clambered up the steps to the front porch. "Oh, Lydi, it is so good to see you! I miss you." She carefully laid the bundle on Lydi's lap and gave her a warm hug.

"Thank you for walking over, Ethel. Please have a seat in William's rocker. He seems to think I should be outside in the fresh air much of the time lately." She smiled to herself, thinking of just last week when she had been kept in the warm confines of the house. The new plans suited her just fine. "How are things at school?"

"Mabel and Lilly and Julia all sent letters for you." She patted the large envelope that was tucked into one of the *Annals of Internal Medicine* publications that she had brought from Miss Johnston at school. "The advanced classes are not the same without you." Then she grinned mischievously and patted her friend's knee. "I think Benjamin misses you, too. I see him look over at your desk sometimes, like he is thinking of you. And, each day he gathers your homework to send with Michael."

Lydi blushed and shook her head at her friend's teasing, her insides warming to match her face. She grasped for a different subject. "I trust Michael is doing well, keeping up with his classes?"

"Yes, he is doing fine, though he seems quieter when you are gone. Probably worried about his sister. Emma seems to have turned her attentions to Benjamin's little brother."

Lydi laughed, remembering Emma's overt flirting with her brother. "Michael has no time for girls, at least not yet!"

Ethel continued updating her friend on school happenings. "Do you remember Damien Crook, Lem's friend who went to school here for just a short time?"

How could she ever forget Damien? He and Lem had bullied Michael and every young student in school. "Yes, I remember. Did he stop at school again?"

"Yes. Miss Johnston was very kind to him. I think she felt sorry for him, having such a bad situation at home. Then his dad was in prison, still is, I think. He stopped at school on his way to Fort Benning in Georgia. He told the class that the army had stepped up training programs. Rumor has it among ranks that our country is preparing for possible involvement in the war in Europe." After she had spoken, Ethel fretted that she was adding more worries to Lydi's already uncertain life. Both girls had heard horror stories of the Great War that had ended in 1918.

"I do have happy news, too, Lydi. Miss Johnston and Greg Christleton are to be married this summer! Little Vicky is so excited. She reminds us almost daily that she and Ricky will have a mommy again soon." Ethel's eyes lit with excitement.

Lydi clasped her hands and looked at her friend expectantly. "Go on, Ethel. There is something else you want to tell me."

"Oh, Lydi, I have been asked to take over for Miss Johnston. I will begin teaching the fall term! I am thrilled, but also a bit nervous. I don't know if I will be able to handle all the classes, and I also need to finish normal school. That is part of the board's requirement for me if I accept the position."

Lydi reached for her friend's hand. "You will be an excellent teacher, Ethel. Of course you must take the job, though it will be strange to call you Miss Bollinger."

Ethel stood then and brushed the wrinkles out of her skirt. "I must be getting home to help Mother and Esther." She pulled on her gloves and wrapped a knitted scarf around her neck. "Oh, I almost forgot. I have not heard from Billie for a while. Mr. Swanson at the newspaper office told Mother that he had read in the *Rocky Mountain News* that there have been labor strikes in the mines, even some violence. I do hope Billie's family will be all right."

"Oh, no. Thanks for letting me know. I will write her soon."

Ethel bent to hug her friend. "Is there anything I can do to help you, Lydi? We keep praying that you will gain more movement each day."

Lydi looked up earnestly. "Yes, Ethel, there is something you can do."

Promises in Courage

CHAPTER 34

IF WISHES WERE SHEEP

Milk stool in place, William leaned his head gently into the warm hip joint of the gentle Jersey milk cow. Bessie had been around for a while, but she was as dependable as daylight and gave the richest milk in the county. The housewives who frequented Chet's mercantile attested to that, and were willing to pay a few extra pennies for the cream that William and Geoffrey separated from the milk. "Makes the best whipped cream you ever tasted on top of pumpkin pie!" they said.

Bessie stood quietly chewing her cud. The small streams of milk swished into the bucket and the froth rose as William skillfully brought forth Bessie's gift, enjoying the unique aroma of fresh milk that rose like steam in the cold morning air. A feeling of contentment settled over the man and he reveled in the goodness of life.

All of a sudden his reverie was interrupted by a commotion outside the barn. What was that noise? It sounded like the frightened bleat of a baby lamb, combined with the unsteady answering "Baaaaa" of an adult sheep that was running. *How could this be?* The sheep were all out in the south pasture. The sound grew closer. He sat the milk pail aside, gave his favorite cow an apologetic pat on the rump and hurried outside the barn door. Geoffrey, who was also working in the barn, was right behind him. What the two brothers saw as they turned toward the house made them stop in their tracks.

Michael was running as fast has his little legs would carry him with a wriggling, blanket-wrapped bundle in his arms. A small white head kept peeking from the blanket. Beside Michael ran his beloved sheep, Dottie, voicing sheep-words of comfort to her new lamb.

The two older men stood, hands in coverall pockets, and watched as the boy and the mother sheep scurried up the steps, onto the porch and up to the front door. Michael pushed open the door. "Lydi!" he called, and disappeared inside, along with the baby and its mother. Shaking their heads, they looked at each other and grinned, both aware of the boy's intention.

"Well, Brother, Lydi will be walking before we know it," William slapped Geoffrey's back as they turned back to their chores in the barn. "She has been making incredible progress recently."

"That she has, good William," Geoffrey answered and rubbed his hands together. He was positive his new liniment concoction was the main reason for her swift recovery.

Promises in Courage

CHAPTER 35

MICHAEL'S HEALING GIFT

"Lydi, Lydi! I have a surprise for you!" Michael found Lydi in Grandma's sewing room, sitting at the Singer machine, attempting to push the treadle with her right foot. She carefully turned her body to face her brother.

"Oh, Michael! Dottie had her lamb! It is so adorable." Lydi reached into the blanket to rub the baby lamb's head after Michael deposited the parcel directly onto her lap. She hugged the little creature close to her body. Dottie looked from Michael to Lydi to her newborn lamb. The mother sheep rubbed her head on Lydi's knees, bleated softly and looked up into the girl's eyes.

"She was just born last night," Michael explained, the excitement shining in his little-boy eyes. "I wanted you to be the first one to see her," he beamed. "She's a girl, and you can name her if you want." He scratched behind the lamb's small white ear that dipped forward at the sight of her mother.

Lydi thought for a few seconds in happy silence. "Sammy. If it is all right with you, I would like to name her Sammy after the little girl that was my roommate in the polio ward at the hospital."

"Sammy. I like it. It goes just fine with 'Star,' her sister's name," Michael nodded with a bright smile. "Do you like that name for your baby, Dottie?" He turned to his oldest sheep. She baaaa'd quite loudy and began to nibble Michael's coat sleeve. Both children giggled.

"Well, I suppose I'd better be getting these two back home to the barn, before the baby gets too cold." Michael began to re-wrap the waggling lamb in the blanket. He hugged her into his arms and started for the front door.

"Thank you, Michael," Lydi called to her brother. "That was such a thoughtful thing to do, bring the baby for me to see, and let me name her."

"Aw, it was nothing," the boy said as he turned back. His eyes widened as he saw that his sister was standing. "Wow! It's a miracle!" he blurted. "I knew the baby lamb would help you get better."

Promises in Courage

CHAPTER 36

THE INVITATION

Anna's forehead creased with worry lines as her old pickup bounced over the rough road to the schoolhouse. Miss Johnston had left word at the mercantile that she was to stop on her way home from work. She hoped Michael was not having problems. Since Lydi had contracted polio, the young boy seemed more subdued, almost withdrawn compared to his usual energetic self. She heaved a heavy sigh, remembering how the children had lost their childhood when their father had died, and now Lydi's polio was added to the trials. Anna parked next to Miss Johnston's car and walked up the steps to the building.

The concerned mother knocked lightly, then pushed the door open. "Sally, it's Anna," she announced as she walked through the entry into the classroom. Student drawings and hand-written reports covered the wall behind the teacher.

Miss Johnston stood and extended her hand with a warm smile. "Thank you for coming on such short notice, Anna."

"No problem. Lydi tells me that you have wedding plans this summer. Congratulations!" She gave her friend a hug. "We are so excited for you and Greg and the twins."

"Thank you, Anna." The teacher beamed. "I have exciting news for your family, also. Come sit here by my desk." She reached for a letter that laid open in front of her and handed it to her friend. "Lydi scored in the top ten students in the Iowa Scholar Examination." She waited a moment for the statement to sink in. "The awards, which include a $100 check, will be presented at the capitol building on

April 26. This is a fantastic honor, Anna. I am so proud of her."

"Oh, my." Anna sat, incredulous, staring at the letter.

"Your family and any guests who wish to accompany the winner are invited to attend the ceremony. The school board has given me permission to close school for the day." Miss Johnston studied the woman next to her, unsure of her reaction as she thought of her child's disability. "Anna, Greg and I can help. You may ride to Des Moines with us if you wish, and we can help with the wheelchair."

An unsettled look crossed the woman's face, as though she had not thought of the wheelchair, of Lydi's paralysis. Finally she breathed in and replied. "Thank you for your kind offer, Sally, but I know Ma and William will want to take her." All of a sudden, a smile lit her face. "I think it will all work out just fine." She stood then and clasped the teacher's hand. "Thank you for encouraging Lydi. It has made a huge impact."

Throughout the drive home, Anna planned. First she would tell Ma and William and Geoffrey. Then Michael, if he could keep a secret.

Promises in Courage

CHAPTER 37

LYDI'S REFLECTION

Letter in her hands, Lydi sat in stunned silence. "I cannot believe this. My examination scored in the top ten. It just is not possible," she stammered as she re-read the words.

"'Course, it's possible, Lydi. I knew you'd win it all along," Michael responded with a brother's pride. "You're smart. You read everything, books and medical stuff. You know about things most kids haven't even studied yet."

Resolutely, the girl folded the letter and set it on the table. "I cannot accept the award money. That hundred dollars was intended to be used for college." Her voice quavered. "I do not know if I will ever be able to attend college." Her face turned up to William. "What hope do I have of ever being a doctor? I still cannot walk alone, and you can hardly come to college with me."

The older gentleman who had grown to love his wife's grandchildren like his own, reached for the girl's hand. "Lydi, consider how much progress you have made. Yes, it has transpired in small steps, but you are standing. Each day your leg muscles gain more strength. Remember, even Dr. Heisze believed you would walk."

Eyes flooding with tears, she looked at each of her loved ones, who waited quietly, having anticipated her reaction. They were ready to encourage her. "I will not accept this award from Governor Wilson unless I can walk to the podium to receive it."

Promises in Courage

CHAPTER 38

BILLIE'S LETTER

Lydi opened the door for Ethel as her friend scrambled up the porch steps. "Is everything all right, Ethel? I saw you running up the driveway."

"I know it is not my night to visit, but I could not wait until Friday. I got a letter from Billie and we are worried about her family." Catching her breath, Ethel produced the neatly opened letter from her dress pocket and the girls hurried in to the davenport. Lydi first met her friend's gaze, then unfolded the letter and began to read:

Baldwin, Colorado
March 12, 1940

Dear Ethel,

I am writing this in haste, partly because I don't know when I will get the chance to write again, and partly because I just need to tell someone. Pa and Ma don't know it, but I overheard them talking late last night. They don't usually keep things from us girls, but knowing what will be happening, they might be afraid that Dru or me won't be able to keep our secret.

Ma and Pa and Dru and I will not be living here much longer. There has been serious trouble at the mines. A few miners went on strike because of the low wages and dangerous working conditions. The coal company brought in cheap labor, mostly Irish immigrants, to replace the strikers. These men were not informed that they were displacing striking miners. They did not know about the dangers in the mines. The strikers, and some of the other men, hate these new workers and call them "scabs." What a horrible name! They were bullied and harassed, and some workers refused to team with them. Fights broke out outside the mine. Strikers threatened the immigrant workers, their families, and anyone who sided with them.

Pa could not put up with anyone being treated so unfairly. He befriended some of the new workers and tried to help them learn safe mining procedures, but a slab of rock crashed on his friend, Mr. MacCallery. Pa tried to warn him, to yell at him to move, but he just froze. Pa figured he probably did not understand English. His leg was broken so he is not able to work in the mines.

His daughter, Erin, has been trying to earn money. She has become my friend and I let her wash the neighbor's windows. She is paid only a dime each time, but she is still grateful. I sort of missed putting those dimes in my piggy bank at first, but I told myself I don't have to put food on our table.

Pa said that some of the seams in the mine are running dry and they have to work harder to find coal. Some of it is being consumed by underground fires that rage through old mine workings. Conditions will just get worse, he thinks, and it won't be safe in the mines or in our little camp.

Then Pa told Ma about his plan, and that is how I know we will be moving. He and Mr. MacCallery are going to try and find mine work in Washington. It is not safe for us to just pack up and leave in broad daylight. There are guards about, and there have been several shootings in the last few weeks. On pay day, there are extra sentries all around the mining camp. Pa said they figure if the men are going to walk out, they will do it with money in their pocket. After that night, the mine police do not patrol because they think no one will leave being owed a paycheck. So, Pa is going to pay his debts and work a few days so they don't suspect him of moving out. Then we are going to pack only what we can carry and leave during the night. It is 20 miles to Gunnison and the train. Hopefully some local farmer will give us a ride.

So, my dear cousin, the next time I write, it will be from somewhere in Washington! At least I hope so. I am worried that we will get caught and guards will try and stop us. Or, what if Mr. MacCallery cannot walk with his broken leg?

I am sorry I have been so involved with my problems I have not even inquired about you and Esther. Will you be starting your first teaching position this fall? I do wish you the very best.

Please greet Lydi for me. I hope by now her arms and legs are working as they should. I will come back to Iowa someday, and I intend to see her again. This time we will walk together. I want to learn all about her road to recovery, which I pray is happening.

My love to all of you. I will miss your letters.

Love,

Your cousin Billie

Promises in Courage

CHAPTER 39

WILLIAM APPLESEED

"I cannot believe these sticks will actually grow into apple trees." Lydi held the wrapped bundles of scions that she and William had cut and wrapped back in February. "They look dead to me!"

"Very gently, try bending one of them," William guided. "You notice they are flexible. If they were dead branches, they would snap quite easily. No, Lydi, there is still life in these cuttings. We took them when they were dormant. I stashed them under layers of straw next to the barn, which until recently, was covered with snow. They have been kept cool and moist. At this point, if we can carefully attach them to a parent tree, both the tree and the scion will break dormancy, the scion will attach to the rootstock, and we will have a brand new apple tree."

"It just seems like a miracle." Lydi sighed as she gazed up into the stark branches of the apple tree before them.

"Many things in nature are miraculous, Lydi. Grafting is a fairly simple, inexpensive way to propagate fruit trees, so we can have more trees, and yes, it is truly fascinating. Are you ready to attempt your first graft, young lass?"

Lydi watched and listened as William demonstrated each step. "A sharp knife is essential. Mine is a small knife that I use for nothing but grafting." He wiped it clean with a rag, then moved to a row of two-foot rootstock that he and Geoffrey had rooted and planted nearly a year ago. Lydi followed close behind the man, but held onto the large tree branches for support. William stopped at the first small tree in the row, which also looked like a stick, only longer than the scions. "If you have knowledge of the science behind grafting, you can experiment with different rootstock and different grafts, and you can attempt the process almost any time of the year. I have learned over the years that we have the highest success rate when we graft early in the spring onto stock planted in the orchard, as we are doing today."

Producing the wrapped bundles of scions from the burlap sack that he and Lydi had prepared months previously, William selected a "Chieftain" scion. Lydi eased down on her hands and knees and watched. He trimmed the scion stick to six inches, noting to the girl that there were three buds on that scion, which would, potentially, shoot out small branches when the weather warmed. With the sharp knife the man then cut the bottom of the scion at an angle so it looked like a wedge. He then cut off the rootstock to about six inches and made a cut, which matched the cut on the scion.

"The basic principal that must be followed in grafting is that the cambium layer of the scion must be in direct contact with the cambium layer of the rootstock. The cambium is the circulation system of the tree. It controls the merging and growing, which is what we want to happen here." The farmer showed Lydi the cambium layers on both small branches. "It is the greenish-white layer that is directly under the bark and circles the heartwood of the tree." He pressed the pointed scion against the rootstock. When pressed together the plant looked much like it had before William trimmed both branches. "Now we must attach the two parts together firmly, with cambium layers matching, and seal the cut." He wrapped a flat band around the full length of the wedge cut and tied it snuggly. "Once we graft all of these infant trees, I will bring out some melted beeswax and coat each of the splices. We want to protect them from air and moisture until they meld together and begin to grow."

Lydi rolled to a sitting position near the tree, her legs straight out in front of her. She looked up at Grandpa William. "I think I understand the grafting process, but why not just let the little trees grow?

Why do we need to attach a branch from a different tree?"

"Excellent inquiry, Lass! These rootstocks are mostly from the old Whitney crabapple tree in the back yard. The small apples make delicious pickles and are fun to munch on early in the season, but your grandmother would not appreciate having hundreds of small apples. The scion we attach determines the variety of apple, so we can grow a much larger apple with more desirable flavor that keeps well into the winter."

The girl's eyes lit up at the thought of fresh, juicy apples at Christmas, but then she had another thought. "Then why don't we just plant trees of the larger apples in the first place? Why must the root part be different?"

"Another superb question! The rootstock determines the size that the tree will become and how hardy it will be. These trees must endure our harsh Iowa winters. The crabapple stock is definitely rugged. You will witness the process as these small miracles grow." The gentleman smiled proudly at the inquisitive girl. "Now, it is your turn."

William stood back as Lydi worked on the next rootstock, then after she finally felt satisfied with her work, she crawled to the next one. They had discussed her crawling a few days ago, and agreed that it might assist in her healing. After all, babies crawled before they walked, William had stated. Possibly the brain learned in that order. The young girl was definitely making progress. He did not tell her that he and Geoffrey and Christina had agreed that once she stood and walked on her own, no matter how slowly, she should move back to her home to continue her recovery. Her mother and brother's love would add to her incentive.

An arctic gale swept through the valley and snaked over the hill where the orchard lay next to the sheep pasture. Ominous dark clouds amassed in the west. A storm was coming. William could feel it in his bones.

Promises in Courage

CHAPTER 40

CHOICES

A monstrous blast of wind slammed into the north side of the house. Lydi heard it howl down the chimney, rattling the shiny black pipes. Then there was a pounding sound on the roof, like stones crashing down. She rushed to the window. Small pellets clattered against the glass, then slithered down in tiny wet rivulets.

An ice storm! Lydi paced slowly through the house, walking from chair to wall to dresser, using each object for support. Grandma and William had driven to Mother's to check on the pasture fences. She and Geoffrey were to follow when he had finished the chores. The pickup stood, ready to go, in the front yard. Why was Geoffrey taking so long?

William had mentioned last night at supper that he thought AmyBelle would soon deliver her calf. Geoffrey would certainly check on her in the barn. Possibly she was having problems.

Lydi finished the breakfast dishes, wiped the counters and table and filled the huge teakettle which sat on the warming burner of the kitchen cook stove. She swept the floor, though her mind was on the weather outside. An hour passed and Geoffrey had still not come in from the barn. Next to the front door on the hall tree she saw her flannel-lined coveralls and hat. Should she go out and check on Geoffrey? Maybe he needed help with the calf. She thought of her weak leg muscles that were just beginning to recover. What help could she possibly bring? A wave of helplessness washed over her. Why did the polio have to weaken her so?

At last she opened the front door and looked outside. The ice pebbles had changed to rain, but it was just cold enough that the rain froze as it hit every surface. The porch and steps gleamed with a thick coating of ice. Again, Lydi thought of Geoffrey. Had something happened to him? AmyBelle was a gentle Jersey cow, but she had heard stories of how cows became mean when they had calves. What if the dear man was lying there in the barn? What if he needed help? She could not stop worrying.

Lydi grasped the hall tree and lifted her winter gear from the hooks. She had to sit to get her legs into the pants, but after what seemed like forever, her stockinged feet pushed out the bottom. Hat tugged down almost to her eyes, the girl slipped on her boots and mittens and again opened the front door. The ice glared up at her, as if daring her to step on it.

It won't do if I fall and have to be rescued, she thought. She carefully lowered her body down and crawled out the front door. It rubbed against her side, then banged shut behind her. Turning around, the girl began to back down the three wooden steps, both knees resting on one, then she slid to the next, pausing at the bottom. Could she possibly walk on this ice? Could she get to the barn?

The pickup. It was parked about ten yards away. With a small sense of satisfaction that at least she was adept at crawling, she maneuvered to the back bumper. Pulling herself up, the girl used the vehicle as a buttress to gain a clear view of the barn. She reached for the door handles, then the mirror, and finally rested her hands on the front hood, just next to the windshield. What she saw made her heart pound with fear.

Geoffrey's brown cap with the fur-lined ear flaps skittered across the ice! The wind pushed it closer. She peered through the freezing mist. A dark form lay on the frozen glaze a few feet in front of the barn door. Geoffrey! Was that her imagination or was there a pool of red just in front of him?

Thoughts pounded through her brain, the same rate as her heartbeat. She could crawl to dear Geoffrey, but what good would she be when she got there? She would not be able to help him up or get him to the house. No, she needed help. Crawling or even her slow walking to Mom's, if she could do it, would take too long. It could be too late by the time she got there. At once she thought of the pickup that supported her. She worked her way back to the driver's door. Grabbing the steering wheel with both hands, the girl struggled to pull herself inside and sit.

The horn! Possibly Grandma and William would hear. She pressed down hard on the circle in the center of the steering wheel. Five, ten long honks. She stared at the road that led back from her mom's farm, willing the car to appear. More blasts on the horn.

Hands clenching the wheel, Lydi thought of Geoffrey's suggestion that she learn to drive. "Every farm girl should master control of all farm implements," he had asserted as they had prepared to drive to town one day for supplies. Then he had explained each step. "The key is here in the ignition. Before you turn it, though, you must push the clutch all the way down with your left foot and hold it there." Lydi had listened halfheartedly, for at the time, she doubted if she would ever have the strength in her legs.

Frantically, she tried to recall his instructions. "With the clutch all the way down, you then turn the key forward and just lightly press the gas pedal with your right foot. The engine will turn and you should hear it start. Then you put it in gear and slowly release the clutch."

A hopeful scan of the road still revealed no approaching vehicle. No help coming yet.

Lydi pressed her left foot down on the clutch. Was she strong enough to push it all the way down? Right hand shaking, she managed to turn the key. Nothing. She scooched farther ahead on the seat. Somehow, she had to push the clutch pedal all the way down to the floor. Her legs felt weak and tired. She closed her eyes and turned her head upward, whispering a desperate plea for help, for she knew she could not do this on her own.

Finally, filled with determination, the girl drew in a huge breath. She pressed her left foot down as hard as she could and quickly worked the key. The engine turned! Then died.

The gas. Geoffrey had said to push just a little on the gas. Left foot still pushing in the clutch, she pressed down on the gas pedal with her right foot, and again turned the key. The engine roared to life.

The old farmer had explained the use of the gear-shift. She shoved the lever forward to what she thought was the "1" for first, or low gear. Now, she recalled, SLOWLY lift up on the clutch. At once the vehicle lurched forward. Then it stopped. Again, she started the engine. Again, she let the clutch release, easier this time. The pickup was moving! In spurts and stops the vehicle slowly moved through the yard to the back drive to Mom's.

She had driven only a few yards when she heard wild beeping. William's car careened down the road. It slid from side to side on the glacial surface, but soon turned into the yard and veered in next to her. Lydi sat inside the pickup, which had stopped when her foot miraculously pushed the clutch down.

William jumped out of the car and ran to her, as fast as the treacherous ice would allow. Lydi opened the door and yelled, "Geoffrey! At the barn. I think he's hurt." Her grandfather rushed back to his car and skidded to the barn, sliding to a stop next to his brother's still form.

Lydi turned off the pickup engine, cautiously slid off the seat and planted her feet on the ice-speckled ground. Holding the side of the pickup she started to the barn, but stopped with a gasp when she saw Geoffey's blood-streaked face as William carefully lifted his brother to his feet.

Geoffrey seemed to be conscious, but he struggled to move his legs, and his head rolled to the side as he leaned on William and they made their way to the waiting car. William strained to push Geoffrey into the passenger seat and then hurried to the driver's side. His worried eyes sought Lydi's and he sent her a quick nod before climbing in.

The car engine roared to life. Still clinging to the pickup, Lydi watched as wheels spun and the car swerved wildly to the lane.

Promises in Courage

CHAPTER 41

ADDLED?

The dark clouds gave way to the sun, its brilliant beams bouncing off the icy ground and reaching back to the sky, glistening like a million diamonds. The dazzling white rays transformed the frozen façade to dark pools. Even from inside the house, Grandma and Lydi heard the water dripping from the roof. They busied themselves with preparing supper, though neither spoke. Worry loomed over them. Geoffrey's blood-coated head kept flashing through Lydi's thoughts.

Finally, the older woman began dressing for chores. "I am going to start the milking, just in case

William does not make it home." She did not mention Geoffrey, aware of Lydi's anguish, but not wishing to instill false hope.

"I will help." Lydi stated simply, hoping her grandmother would not object.

Just as they were about to head out the door, they spotted William's pickup as it turned from the road to the driveway, slowly angling around puddles and potholes. They rushed outside as William exited and walked to the passenger side. He opened the door and reached in to assist Geoffrey.

Relieved to see both men returning, the women rushed to William's side as Geoffrey leaned into his brother, one arm around his shoulder mumbling something about William aiming for every bump in the road. Lydi rushed to the man's other side and draped his arm around her shoulder. Christina's eyes met William's as they walked.

Ambling unsteadily, Geoffrey beamed a lopsided grin down at Lydi, then slowly turned his head to William. "I told you, Brother, I look so dashing with my stitches. The dark line over my brow makes me even more debonair. Women are going to flock to my side."

William rolled his eyes upward, though his wife detected a slight twinkle. "The good doctor assured us there was no brain damage. I fear that his diagnosis was woefully mistaken. The patient's mind is obviously addled."

Once inside, everyone helped Geoffrey remove his wraps and settle into the chair next to the stove. After a few moments of bickering with the injured man who insisted he should help with the chores, William and Christina headed outside and Lydi remained to watch Geoffrey.

The man at last leaned his head back, closed his eyes, and blew out an exhausted sigh. "Lydi, you undoubtedly saved my life today. I sincerely thank you."

The young girl's eyes flooded with tears of gratitude that the dear man was still alive, and her throat constricted with so much emotion she could not speak.

The old gentleman opened his eyes and smiled in understanding. Then he winked at her, though he gave a slight wince as the stitches pulled. His head still back, he turned it from side to side ever so slightly, his face beaming in spite of the pain. "Lydi, AmyBelle had twins!"

Promises in Courage

CHAPTER 42

HOME!

"Come on, Lydi! You have to come to the barn." Michael grabbed his sister's hand and earnestly pulled her out the front door. "I thought you'd never come home! Dottie and Star have missed you, and little Sammy has grown since you held her."

"Hold on, Michael. I can only walk so fast!" Lydi laughed tolerantly as she tried to keep up with the boy, sharing his excitement of being home again.

"Sorry, Lydi. I keep forgetting you can't walk real fast yet." His pace slowed, but not his chatter. "Pretty soon William and Geoffrey will bring AmyBelle and her twin calves back. They said you can bottle feed the calves. And going out to the barn every day will help you walk better for when you get your award from the governor." Realizing he was pulling her again, the boy stopped and turned back. "That is, if you want to. If we save part of AmyBelle's milk and give it to the calves, we can still have some fresh milk for us."

The young girl smiled as the two continued down the path, remembering the milkings and the cow's rich cream that Grandma had taken to Chet's mercantile to sell. "I will gladly feed the little calves." Lydi answered knowing she would get plenty of help.

Michael unlatched the door to the barn and stood back impatiently as the young girl shuffled in. They were greeted by the bleating of three sheep. Most would have perceived the sound as a cacophony, but to Lydi it was a harmonious melody. Heads pushed through the wooden fence. Lydi haltingly bent down and buried her fingers in their thick fur. She leaned her forehead to each sheep in turn, savoring the softness and the wooly smell.

Michael saw the tears pooled in her eyes. Again he grabbed his sister's hand. "Now, you've gotta come over here and sit. I've got a surprise for you." He gestured to the pile of clean straw nestled against the store room wall. "You wait right here. And close your eyes."

Wondering what her brother had up his sleeve, she shook her head affectionately, then looked down and shut her eyes tightly. She could hear soft steps on the wooden ladder that led up to the hay-mow. A few seconds later her brother's boots plodded down again, more slowly this time, one step at a time. At last he reached the bottom and she felt him coming toward her.

"Keep your eyes shut." He stopped in front of her and delicately placed something on her lap.

"Oh!" Lydi let out a startled breath as she felt tiny claws prickle through her dress. "It is so tiny!" Delighted, she watched as the bitty kitten stood on shaky paws and blindly stumbled forward, turning its head from side to side, sniffing the hands that encircled it. Abruptly, the creature emitted a frantic "MEW" that seemed far too loud for such a small animal. Lydi carefully lifted the kitten with both hands and held it close. Still, its nose searched and it wobbled about, crying pathetically.

Suddenly, there was a muffled, clicking sound and both children turned to watch a gray tabby cat gracefully tread down the same steps Michael had descended moments ago. She watched warily as Lydi snuggled her kitten. The mother cat sauntered to Michael, rubbed against his legs, and purred. He reached down and scratched under her whiskers as she leaned into his hand. Then she peered up at him and meowed. "It's all right, Girl. I just had to show your baby to Lydi. She will love you both."

"They are adorable, Michael. I cannot believe you managed to keep them a secret." Lydi smiled, remembering the carving he had made her and how much her brother loved to talk.

"I wanted it to be a surprise."

"Mama Kitty is probably worried about her baby," said Lydi observing the cat, which obviously still considered her an intruder.

"I'll take the kitten back up." Michael lifted the kitten to his shoulder and was soon back at his sister's side. The mother cat left as soon as she heard her baby calling from the haymow above.

"What do you call the mother cat, Michael? I think she needs a name."

"Actually, she's got a name. Geoffrey brought her over a few weeks ago. He said to be sure and keep her in the barn and give her food and water. I didn't know then she was in the family's way. I worried about her that first night, but the next morning when I opened the door, there were two dead rats, layin' right next to each other. It was like she left a present for me.

"Since she moved in, I have not seen one live rat. So, I decided on the perfect name for her." He grinned at his sister, then looked down sheepishly as he rubbed the toe of his boot through the straw-laced dirt floor.

"I named her 'Killer.'"

Promises in Courage

CHAPTER 43

THE GREATEST GIFTS

Lydi smoothed the shiny cotton print of her skirt as the car reached the outskirts of Des Moines. Mom had come home from work two weeks ago and announced that Louise and Chet at the mercantile had insisted that she have a new dress for the event. Grandma had sewn it from a Simplicity pattern that cost a nickel. The skirt and matching bolero were navy blue with swirls of silvery white spattered throughout like tiny sunbursts. The crisp, white collar and sleeves of the blouse stood out against the dark blue dress. For a few moments the girl felt almost elegant, but her confidence was soon displaced by nerves, and silently she hoped she would not embarrass her loved ones today.

Geoffrey pulled out his pocket watch and gave it a quick glance as he maneuvered around a slow-moving farm truck. "It is most propitious that I did the driving today. We will arrive in good time, indubitably due to my accomplished skill."

William, who sat in the back seat with Lydi placed between him and Grandma, shook his head in feigned exasperation. "Well, it is most fortunate that Lydi is alive to receive her award, considering the breakneck speed to which she has been subjected." He patted Lydi's shoulder with one hand, then winked over at his wife. Finally, he sighed dramatically and made a show of laboriously extricating his fingers from the interior side panel of the car. Michael looked back from the front seat and stifled a giggle. Geoffrey drove on, oblivious it seemed to the lighthearted teasing around him.

For weeks Lydi had pictured this day in her mind. She was apprehensive about walking up to receive her award from the governor, but hoped that she would be able to sit close and possibly have something to reach for, a chair or podium, if she needed it. Thankful that they had arrived a bit early, the girl was anxious to get inside to prepare herself.

Geoffrey held the front door of the capitol building open while the others entered, Lydi clutching her mother's arm. Immediately, they were greeted by a prim young woman in a dark suit and heels. William and Geoffrey removed their hats and each politely bowed. She smiled warmly and addressed Lydi. "Are you one of our ten honorees today?"

Lydi flushed shyly and managed to smile back. "Yes, I guess I am."

The woman strode to Lydi's side and began escorting her to a side room. "You come with me to the library. Before the ceremony you will get to meet Governor Wilson and Miss Bayir and Dr. Ann Flanders." She turned back to the others. "There is an usher in the Conference Room. She will show you the reserved seating area." Lydi hesitated and glanced back at her family. Nods and smiles of encouragement reassured her.

In the library, the three adults shook hands with each young person and welcomed them into the group. At 1:50, ten minutes before the ceremony, the two women spoke to the students, congratulating them on their honors and inspiring them to continue their education after high school. Both emphasized the need for medical professionals in the state of Iowa. Lydi's tension eased slightly and the dream that the polio had shattered began to mend and grow.

At two minutes before 2:00, the same woman who had met Lydi at the door returned to guide the group to the conference room for the awaited award ceremony. "Student winners, after the speeches by our distinguished guests, you will each be called forward to receive your award. Names will be called in random order. You will walk up to accept your gift, and then go back to the greeting line where family and friends will be waiting for you. Now, please follow me."

Lydi's heart started pounding and her throat constricted with panic. The procession entered the room and filed to the front row of chairs facing the podium and the seated dignitaries. In her panic she did not even scan the room for her family.

She sat in the hard wooden chair, feet planted firmly, hands clasped together. Miss Bayir remarked of the importance of higher education, especially for women. The doctor reiterated her exhortation. Soon the governor stood to acknowledge the young people's accomplishments and it was time to present the honors.

Lydi stared at the floor, the path that led to the governor's platform. Feeling wetness under her arms, she hoped her bolero would not betray her. The first name was called and a young man from Underwood bounded up confidently. With each name, Lydi grew more distressed. *What if I can't get up from my chair? What if I stumble on the way?*

Fear tangled around her heart as she worried frantically. *What if I lose my courage and sit here as though I was still paralyzed?*

It seemed like everyone around her had received their gift, shaken hands with their family and returned to their seat. Her turn had to be soon.

"Lydi Anna Andersson. Lydi hails from Chaucer Township School Number Seven near Canterbury.....

Unaware that she had even stood up on her own, she found herself moving forward, one slow step at a time, willing her legs to press on. Time seemed to stand still, and she was certain her journey was taking hours. At last, Lydi reached the officials. Amid handshakes and warm smiles, the girl was vaguely aware of accepting an envelope and politely saying thanks. Still in a daze of nerves, she turned back and there was her mother, eyes reflecting her love and pride.

Anna took a step forward and Lydi moved, slowly but steadily, to her awaiting embrace. Neither could find words to express their feelings.

"Good job, Sis. I knew you could do it!" Michael piped up as he stepped forward and wrapped his arms around her.

Then Grandma was smiling into her eyes. "I am so proud of you, Granddaughter."

All at once two little bodies simultaneously flung into her skirt. "You did good, Lydi! Con-gratch-u-lay-shuns." Ricky and Vicky jumped up and down in front of her as Miss Johnston and Greg Christleton shook her hand.

With blurry eyes she took another step and there in front of her stood Benjamin, beaming that winning smile. "Congratulations, Lydi. You certainly deserve this honor." He extended his hand and she stood there, looking into his eyes. Blushing.

"I…..am so glad you came." Realizing she was still holding his hand she blurted "Thank you, Benjamin!" and continued down the line.

She was then wrapped in a faithful hug by Ethel. "Oh, Lydi, best wishes to you, my friend! You walked just fine."

"Thank you for all that you did," Lydi whispered into her friend's ear.

Geoffrey stood next in line. He swallowed and cleared his throat as his love and gratitude for this young girl overcame him. Lydi smiled as she glanced up at the bright red scar that lined his eyebrow, then reached up to hug the dear old gentleman.

William patted his brother's back affectionately, for he had never known Geoffrey to be at a loss for words. Then he wrapped his granddaughter in a warm hug. At last he gently took her arm to turn her attention behind them.

A tall man who had been standing back from the group, limped forward.

"Oh! Dr. Heisze! You came here? To see me?"

Strong arms encircled her and he rested his head on top of hers. "Lydi Andersson, I knew you could do it."

Suddenly, the dam of pent-up tears burst. Surrounded by the others, the doctor and the girl stood, holding onto each other, tremoring with broken sobs.

After a few moments the doctor placed his hands on the girl's shoulders, stood back and looked down at her tear-streaked face. "Lydi. I knew that day you left the hospital that you would walk again." Then he extended his elbow for her hand. Together the man and the girl started slowly back to the chairs, one with a limp and one unsteady on her feet. At last he turned and looked into her eyes. "And today, Lydi, I am certain that someday you will be a doctor."

Promises in Courage

JOURNAL OF LYDI ANNA ANDERSSON

MAY 31, 1940

I walked to school today! It was the first time I walked there since the day I got polio. For a while I stayed home and kept up with schoolwork. Later, Mom or Grandpa William or Geoffrey dropped me off every morning and picked me up at the end of the day.

Today was the last day of school; Miss Johnston's last day of teaching before she marries Greg Christleton and becomes a mommy to little Vicky and Ricky. When school starts again in the fall, Ethel will be our teacher. I walked because I needed to know I can do it. My legs ache tonight, but by fall I will be stronger. Milking AmyBelle and gardening and helping Grandpa William with the orchard will all help.

Ethel has not heard from Billie for months. I hope her father has found work in Washington, though I think it would be awful to work in any coal mine. Billie won't be able to come to Iowa again this Christmas, but we can still write letters.

I am almost afraid to look forward to summer or fall or anything because it seems like when I do, something bad happens. Polio almost destroyed my dreams, but, thank God I overcame the paralysis. I had a lot of help from Dr. Heisze, William and Geoffrey and Grandma. Mom and Michael cheered me on and dear Ethel came every week to help me stand.

So I will try and dream again. The check for $100 that I got from the governor is in a savings account at Greg Christleton's bank in Canterbury. First I gave it to Mom, and told her to use it to pay my hospital bills. She smiled and told me the bills had been taken care of. Then she gave me a hug and said that Samantha's bills had been paid, too.

One hundred dollars is a good start for medical school and I will add to it soon. Dr. Evans asked me to work at his office again this summer. Mrs. Evans is expecting a baby any day now and won't be able to assist her husband. When I work at the office, sometimes I get to see Benjamin at his father's pharmacy.

Mom is setting aside money, too. She says the REA is coming through Iowa soon to run electric lines across the country. Then we will have lights and not need to take lamps everywhere. Michael says we need electric lights in the barn, too, if he is going to be a real farmer. He still insists we must have a radio. Mom tries to hide her grin when he mentions it.

So, again I am looking forward. I am dreaming. I hope nothing else gets in the way of my dreams.

L. A. A.

ABOUT THE AUTHOR

DeAnn Kruempel, author of *Promises to Keep, Promises Challenged, and Promises Strengthened,* was born and raised on a farm near De Smet, South Dakota. She has also lived in rural North Dakota and Iowa. For the last 30 years she has worked as a Children's Librarian at schools and public libraries.

The author enjoys working in her orchard, reading and spending time with her family and friends. She lives on an acreage near Logan, Iowa with her cat, Elsa, 12,497 honeybees and 16 chickens, including Little Black Banty.

CREDITS

With sincere gratitude, I dedicate this book to Helen, a polio survivor, and to the memory of Sammy, who fought with such courage.

Special thanks to Helen, Ethel and Billie for the stories.

To my siblings, children, grandchildren and friends: Your support and encouragement are the most wonderful awards I could ever receive.

Thanks to my editors Bruce and Dorothy and to Nathan at Boekerbooks.

Made in the USA
Lexington, KY
03 November 2019